Caught!

With trembling hands, Patsy lifted the saddlebags, slipped open the buckles on one side and looked inside. It was empty. She opened the other side. This pocket had only several newspapers, folded neatly.

On the table by the chair was a coat, hat and small leather case. She took a deep breath, and with trembling fingers, she unlocked the case and lifted the lid.

Inside was only a violin.

"Are you a lover of music as well as of books?" came a loud voice from the doorway.

Patsy spun around. There, with his hands on his hips, was the tall stranger.

He wasn't smiling this time.

Books in the DAUGHTERS OF LIBERTY series
(by Elizabeth Massie)

Published by MINSTREL Books

DAUGHTERS *of* LIBERTY

PATSY AND THE DECLARATION

Elizabeth Massie

A MINSTREL® BOOK

Published by POCKET BOOKS
New York   London   Toronto   Sydney   Tokyo   Singapore

A MINSTREL PAPERBACK *Original*

A Minstrel Book published by
POCKET BOOKS, a division of Simon & Schuster Inc.
1230 Avenue of the Americas, New York, NY 10020

Copyright © 1997 by Elizabeth Massie

ISBN: 0-671-00133-7

First Minstrel Books printing August 1997

10 9 8 7 6 5 4 3 2 1

A MINSTREL BOOK and colophon are registered trademarks of Simon & Schuster Inc.

Cover art by Ernie Norcia

Printed in the U.S.A.

To my son, Brian, with all my love and sincerest wishes for a wonderful, peaceful and joyous life journey. Keep on playin'!

PATSY AND THE DECLARATION

1

"Dorcas certainly does cry a lot!" said twelve-year-old Patsy Black as she watched her mother place her brand-new baby sister into the wooden cradle. "Did I cry that much when I was her age?"

Mrs. Black smiled at Patsy, then patted baby Dorcas gently on the back. Even though it was early morning, the small family bedroom was already hot and sunny. The only relief came from the breeze that had found its way through the open window. "All babies cry, Patsy. You did. Henry did. Nicholas did."

"Even you and Father," Patsy added.

Mrs. Black smiled. "Of course. And Dorcas is

only ten days old. There isn't much of this world she understands yet. She is only now learning who we are."

Patsy gazed at her little sister. Dorcas had bright blue eyes, a fine spray of pale blond hair and a tiny nose. Patsy's own hair was straight and blond, and her nose was short and turned up just a bit. It would be funny if her sister grew up to look just like her. But it might be nice, too.

It was late June and hot both inside and out, but baby Dorcas was properly dressed for an infant. She wore a linen petticoat and gown. On her head was a tiny cap of linen and ribbon, and on her hands were two beautifully sewn mittens, hemstitched and embroidered.

"Sleep now, my girl," said Mrs. Black as she tucked a flannel sheet over the baby. Over the sheet went a white silk blanket, which had been a gift from the Blacks' neighbor, Mrs. Brubaker, at Dorcas's christening the day before at the church.

Patsy helped her mother move the cradle just a little closer to the window. This way, Patsy could sit in the straight-backed chair while she rocked the baby and look out at the blooming roses and the shady oak trees in the tavern's side garden. The window was pushed open as far as it would go, and the wooden Venetian blinds were pulled up, letting in the breeze and the sweet scent of the roses. When she had time between her chores later, Patsy would go sit in the garden with her friend Barbara Layman and play games or dolls. The shade from the trees always helped ease the heat.

Suddenly the bedroom door opened. Patsy's seven-year-old brother, Nicholas, bounded in, clutching a cloth bag of marbles. Mrs. Black held up her finger to keep him from making noise.

Nicholas was short and slim, with blond hair and bright blue eyes. The fair skin of his face was pink with sunburn. "Hello," he said in an almost-quiet voice. "I'm off to play with Robert and Allen down at the marketplace."

"Ho, there," Mrs. Black said. "You have a lesson with the Anderson ladies now. You are to work on your spelling, young man."

Nicholas made a face. "But the boys are waiting outside for me, Mother. They will be angry if I can't play with them. Can't the lesson wait?"

"No, Nicholas. Tell your friends you can join them in an hour or so. Put the marbles away and go to the backyard. Take your slate and pencil."

With a loud sigh, Nicholas opened a drawer in the small table by the window, pulled out his writing tools, then went back out, closing the door behind him.

"Now, Patsy," Mrs. Black said. She took a clean apron from the wardrobe and tied it around her waist. "I will be busy for the next hour. I must make sure Nicholas has emptied the chamber pots and put logs into the fireplaces. We both know he is careless at times. I have to be certain that the Anderson sisters have done the laundry before they tutor your brother. And Katherine needs to know how much to cook for this afternoon's meal."

"Yes, Mother," Patsy said.

"You will sit with Dorcas. And I mean sit. You have nothing pressing but to be with your sister."

"Yes, Mother, I know."

Mrs. Black smoothed her apron and straightened the collar of her gown. Although Patsy's mother was still recovering from Dorcas's difficult birth and had spent the first six days in bed, she was now strong and determined enough to keep her finger on the pulse of the family's business, Black's Tavern. She seemed to enjoy the bustle of the place and the constant activity and excitement going on with the men who were the tavern's patrons.

Mrs. Black opened the bedroom door, which led to the tavern's Red Horse Room. "Rock the baby slowly," she said with a wide grin and a wink. "Dorcas is not as likely to enjoy as rough a ride as Nicholas would!"

"Yes, Mother," Patsy said, laughing. She sat by the cradle and rocked it gently with the toe of her leather shoe. The baby seemed to like the motion of the cradle. At least she wasn't crying anymore. Her tiny eyes began to close. Her baby nose twitched and relaxed. Patsy rocked the cradle and watched as her sister slowly fell asleep.

"Having a baby in the tavern certainly does turn things upside down," Patsy said to herself. "I have little time left to work on my sewing and my letters. I can barely find a spare minute to read. Why, my dolls Sallie Jones and Mrs. Byrd have barely had a glimpse of me since Dorcas was born."

She sighed and rocked the cradle. Many women neighbors and friends had come to visit and help with the baby. Some brought gifts and food. This was kind, and both Mrs. Black and Patsy were thankful. But in spite of the help, life at Black's

Tavern had become very hectic. In addition to her other chores, Patsy had to help change Dorcas's clouts and hold the baby and walk her when she cried, which was often. She had to help the Anderson sisters with the extra loads of baby clothes, stirring them in the laundry pot and hanging them out on the line in the backyard. Babies' clothes were not to be washed with those of the adults, so her mother said. They should always be separate because babies were delicate. But, of course, this made double the work.

"Mother says not to fret," Patsy said to herself. "She said that life will settle down soon enough. In just a few months, there will be time again for books and penmanship. I wonder if she is right."

"Pssst!" came a voice. Patsy looked out of the window. There, with hands on her hips, was Barbara, Patsy's best friend, standing in the side garden. She was a stout girl with curly black hair pinned up under a mobcap and a blue dress already covered with streaks of dirt. Her smile was mischievous and generous. Freckles were sprinkled across her nose and cheeks. Barbara lived on the second floor of the tavern's stable with her father and mother. Her father took care of the stable and the horses of the men who frequented the tavern. Mrs. Layman was a clerk at Boxler's Milliner, several streets over. Barbara helped her father in the stable during the day and helped her mother with women's chores at night. Sometimes Patsy envied the freedom Barbara had. Her father wasn't as particular about Barbara being a lady. She was even allowed to ride her pony, Little Bit, astraddle like a boy!

"What are you up to in there, Patsy?" Barbara asked.

"I'm rocking Dorcas," said Patsy. "I don't have time to play right now. Mother has gone out to attend to the tavern, and I must stay with my sister."

"When will you be able to play, then?" Barbara asked. "Do you know we haven't had time to be Daughters of Liberty since the baby came? How can we be good Patriots if we can't even meet and talk about our plans?"

"Plans?" Patsy said, shaking her head. "I can hardly think straight, I'm so tired. Dorcas cries so much, and at night especially. I wish our family had two rooms instead of only one. Why do babies think it best to cry at three in the morning?"

Barbara grinned. "I don't know. But I do know it's a beautiful day, and until my father comes back from the saddle maker's, I have some time to play. How long until Dorcas is asleep?"

"She nearly is now."

"Can't you come outside while she is sleeping?"

Patsy said, "I can't leave her alone. I have to wait until Mother comes back. Why don't you come in and help me?"

"Help you what?"

"Help me rock her and watch her."

Barbara ran her hand over her chin and said, "I dare not. I'd surely wake her as noisy as I am at times. Come on outside, Patsy. You would hear her cry, as we're just outside the window. And I have something I must show you right away."

"What?"

"Come out and I'll show you. It's something the Daughters of Liberty must know about."

The Daughters of Liberty was a secret organization Patsy and Barbara had formed. They had agreed to watch out for spies in Philadelphia, to pass secret messages and to do deeds of worth to help the Patriots' cause of independence. The only problem was, they had had just one adventure so far. While walking in the street together earlier in the summer, they had found a secret note from a British spy. They had taken it to the State House, where the Continental Congress was meeting. The man who took the note had been grateful. Patsy and Barbara had been very proud of themselves.

But then, with the demands of the new baby, there had been no time to do anything more. There was nothing Patsy would rather do than have a new Daughters of Liberty adventure, but how could she?

"You're a bother," Patsy said, shaking her head at Barbara. "Play by yourself."

"Come outside," Barbara pressed. "We will be as close to the baby as six feet. That should be all right."

Dorcas was sleeping, and it would certainly be easy for Patsy to hear her if she cried. The window was open and the garden was just outside.

"Please?"

"Gracious!" Patsy said. "I suppose I can, but just for a few minutes." She gave the cradle one more gentle push with her foot, then climbed quickly out the window and dropped to the soft grass of the garden. She tugged her apron back straight and put her hands on her hips. "Well, then?"

"See what I've found!" Barbara said. She dropped to the ground, cross-legged. Patsy, always more careful than Barbara when it came to caring for her clothes, tucked her skirt and her feet beneath her as she sat. Mrs. Black would not be pleased if yet again Patsy wound up with grass stains on the fabric. *Boys can be excused for soiling their clothes,* Patsy thought. *Young ladies are supposed to be delicate and docile in their play. Sometimes I think it would be easier to be a boy for the messiness they can get away with!*

"Look." Barbara took a small book from the pocket of her skirt. "It's causing all such turmoil in the city. My father bought a copy and read some aloud to my mother last night when he thought I was sleeping. But I wasn't. I was listening, and knew that the Daughters of Liberty should see it."

Patsy picked up the book. The title seemed harmless enough—*Common Sense.* The name of the man who wrote the book rang with no trace of trouble-making—Thomas Paine. Yet Patsy had heard of this book. As anger at King George had grown in the city of Philadelphia, the book had become very popular. While clearing plates and refilling mugs in the tavern's dining room, Patsy had heard men discuss the book. She'd even seen a volume lying on a stand in one of the tavern's upstairs bedrooms. But as curious as she'd been, she'd not touched it. Andrew Black, Patsy's father, was not keen on his family becoming involved in the debate concerning independence. He didn't tell his children what to think, but Patsy knew he would rather they leave the matter of the struggle with the British to others. Patsy knew that her older brother, Henry, was fascinated with the soldiers he'd seen around the city in their uniforms. She even thought he might have joined up if given approval from his father, but Patsy knew he would never get it. Maybe Henry would join someday soon, with or without Father's permission.

Barbara drew up close to her friend and looked over her arm. "What does it say?" she asked. "I only heard part of it last night, but I want to know it all."

"I will read you a small portion," Patsy said. "But then I must go back in and tend Dorcas."

Barbara nodded, grinning widely. "I wish I could read as well as you, Patsy," she said. Although Barbara had freedoms Patsy did not, it sometimes saddened Patsy that her friend could not read. When she had a chance, Patsy gave her lessons, but it was such an effort for Barbara at times to decipher what was in a book or a newspaper. Some girls were never even taught letters, but Patsy's parents saw that a simple education in reading, writing and calculating would help a woman perform her housewifery duties all the better once she was married. It wasn't that Barbara's parents had anything against a girl learning, they just didn't have the time to be concerned with such things.

Opening the book to the first page, Patsy read, " 'Some writers have so confounded society with government as to leave little or no distinction between them.' "

"I don't understand that," Barbara said. "Tell me what it means."

"I'm not certain," Patsy said.

"Then read another part."

"All right." Patsy flipped several pages. She read, " 'If we will suffer ourselves to examine the component parts of the English constitution, we shall find them to be the base remains of two ancient tyrannies.' "

"Tyrannies!" Barbara said. "I know what that

means. Paine is declaring that the English are oppressing us!"

"Yes," said Patsy. "Mr. Thomas Paine has dared to put in print that the King doesn't care about those of us in the colonies."

"Read on," Barbara said.

Patsy read, " 'There is something exceedingly ridiculous in the composition of Monarchy.' "

"Oooh!" said Barbara. "Now he says the King is ridiculous!"

"He does say that," said Patsy. "Mr. Paine best hide if the King's soldiers invade Philadelphia. He would be caught and hanged for certain."

"For certain," Barbara said. "The man is brave to write such words. If I could write, I would write brave words like those."

"And chance being hanged?"

"I would first practice running very fast and hiding in small places!" Barbara giggled.

Suddenly Patsy sat straight. She thought she had heard a thumping sound inside the bedroom. "Barb, did you hear something?"

"No."

"I heard something inside my family's bedroom."

"No, you didn't. It's only your mother talking

to the Anderson ladies in the backyard," Barbara said. "Now, read some more from the book."

Patsy jumped up. She was supposed to be watching her sister! "No, I must get back inside right away," she said. She tossed the book to Barbara. And then, placing her hands on the window sill, she pulled herself into the bedroom. She brushed herself off and looked into the cradle.

It was empty. Dorcas was gone.

2

"Dear me!" Patsy cried. "Where did Dorcas go?"

Surely her baby sister was too young to get out of the cradle on her own. Someone had taken her away! It wasn't Mother; Mother and Nicholas were both in the backyard. Father and her sixteen-year-old brother, Henry, had gone to the wheelwright's shop.

Who, then, had taken Dorcas?

Her heart pounding, Patsy first searched the bedroom. The baby wasn't under the bed, nor was she behind the wardrobe. Had a tavern visitor taken the baby, to hold her as hostage? These days, people were thinking and doing strange and frightening things. Was her innocent sister being

★ 15 ★

held at this very moment by a Tory as ransom for an arrested British spy?

What am I going to do?

Patsy raced from the bedroom and into the adjoining Red Horse Room. Only two men were there, sitting by the window and smoking their pipes. Neither turned to look at her, and neither had the baby. She went into the hall and gazed anxiously at the men sipping ale in the Ulysses Room. Only a handful were there, and none were in possession of Dorcas.

What shall I do? My sister's missing and it is my fault!

Then a voice called from up the stairs. "Patsy."

Patsy turned and looked. On the landing stood Katherine Ralston, a young woman who cooked and cleaned at the tavern. She held little Dorcas in her arms. With a sigh of relief, Patsy darted up the steps.

"I was afraid she'd been stolen!" Patsy said. "I've heard so much about the men who are loyal to the Crown, and how devious they can be. I thought our Dorcas had been taken hostage!"

Katherine shook her head patiently. But there was a hint of disappointment in her eyes. "You can't leave a child alone, Patsy. I thought you knew that. I returned earlier than planned and stopped by your bedroom a moment ago to see the baby. But when I went inside, there was no one there but poor little Dorcas, fussing. So, I took her upstairs to find you."

"I'm sorry," Patsy said gravely. "Are you going to tell Mother I left her alone?"

"Will you promise never to do it again?"

Patsy nodded vigorously.

Then Katherine said, "Hostage? You have such an imagination, Patsy."

"I know," Patsy said.

The two walked down the steps. "I will watch Dorcas now," Katherine said. "Mrs. Brubaker stopped me in front of her house just a few minutes ago and asked that you come over as soon as possible. She has a chore for you to do, and your mother will not mind that I watch the baby."

"Very well," Patsy said. "And thank you."

Katherine smiled. "Just keep your head, child. It's the best way to stay out of trouble."

Patsy nodded, then opened the large tavern door and went out into the bright June sunlight.

Out on Mulberry Street, the pounding of horses' hooves and the roll of wagon wheels drove clouds of dust into the air like swarms of tiny insects. It had rained a little the night before, leaving the air hot and steamy. Men and women on foot picked their way carefully to avoid the holes and the manure. Two brown horses were tied to the posts in front of Black's Tavern. One belonged to a guest, the other was Mr. Black's horse, Thunder. Patsy gave them both a hearty pat as she went by. They rolled their eyes in her direction, then let their eyelids close. Their tails swished against buzzing flies.

Two men were on the walk where Patsy wanted to go. They were jabbing fingers at each other and yelling. Patsy listened intently as she approached them. Daughters of Liberty needed to be alert.

"We should send them all back to their homes, every member of the Continental Congress!" declared one old man with a white powdered wig on his head. "Our city appears to be the hotbed for rebels with them meeting in the State House everyday and talking about breaking free from England, making decisions for us even though we don't all agree. I say send them home!"

But the second man, younger, with cheeks reddened in anger, said, "We used to be friends, Matthew. And listen to yourself! The Congress is doing us a service, deciding how we can best take care of the nasty situation England has put us in. England doesn't care about us—taxing us, taking away our rights, and now fighting with us—and we shouldn't care about her anymore. I say the Congress is doing the right thing!"

The men were so involved in their yelling that they didn't even notice the blond girl with the pink dress and white mobcap squeezing around them so as not to step in a small puddle of mud from the rain.

I wonder what Mrs. Brubaker wants? Patsy thought as she walked to the house next door and up onto the stoop.

A month ago, Patsy would have dreaded going to Mrs. Brubaker's house. The woman had a reputation for being a nasty, sharp old woman who never had a smile or a kind thing to say. She often complained if Nicholas so much as peered over her garden wall or Patsy sang too loudly in the side garden. She had even accused Patsy of trespassing when the girl fell off the wall into the old woman's yard. And it had been an accident.

But just a little over a week ago, on the day Dorcas was born, Patsy and Barbara had saved Mrs. Brubaker's life. Looking through the old woman's window, they had seen Mrs. Brubaker collapsed on the floor. A quick trip to get the doctor had meant the difference between life and death. Now, Mrs. Brubaker was still gruff and stern, but there was an underlying kindness Patsy had not seen before, and the two of them were becoming good friends.

It took several knocks before Mrs. Brubaker opened her door. She was still recovering from her fall and so was moving slowly and with care. But she was dressed in her finest silk gown covered with flowers and bows, and her silver hair was styled to perfection with a lace cap pinned on top. The woman's tight lined lips twitched in a small smile when she saw it was Patsy who had come to visit.

"I had thought you'd be here sooner," she said, stepping back to let Patsy enter the foyer. "I spoke with Katherine at least ten minutes ago. What kept you, Miss Black?"

Patsy knew the grumbling was only habit. "I'm sorry, Mrs. Brubaker," she said. "I just now heard you needed me for an errand. Katherine couldn't find me. What may I do for you?"

The woman stood as straight as she could and folded her hands gracefully at her waist. "There are a number of items I need and you will go to the shops for me. I will give you several shillings to obtain some borax, cream of tartar, and dried figs at the apothecary. And I've an order to put in with Betsy Ross. I have it here on this slip of paper. And last, the silversmith, Earl Ford, has finished a tray I ordered, and it is to be picked up."

"Yes, ma'am. And is there anything else while I'm about?"

Before Mrs. Brubaker could answer, there was a barking sound from down the hall. A small black-and-white puppy came bounding into the foyer. His short little tail wagged madly, and he jumped up, putting his front paws on Patsy's skirt.

"Hello, there, George!" Patsy said. "You little scoundrel! How have you been behaving for this lady?"

The puppy barked again and wriggled, the nails of his back paws making tiny scratching noises on the polished wood floor.

"Oh, he is a trial, this one," Mrs. Brubaker said. "Never a moment's peace unless he's sleeping. I even caught him trying to dig a new hole beneath the wall in my backyard. I believe he meant to go over and visit you at the tavern."

Patsy laughed. The puppy had belonged to her

not long ago, but had caused nothing but trouble. But recently Patsy and Mrs. Brubaker had agreed to be co-owners of the dog because Mrs. Brubaker was so taken with his boundless affection. Patsy was glad the old woman had something that loved her without condition.

"Little George is glad to see you," Mrs. Brubaker said. "And I believe he could use some time to run outside, to stretch his legs and see other faces besides that of an old woman. You will take him with you, Miss Black, but mind he doesn't get away."

Oh, dear, I don't want to, Patsy thought. She knew what trouble the little dog could be. Holding on to a leash made walking very difficult, as he was constantly tugging and jumping.

"You will take him?" Mrs. Brubaker repeated.

"Yes, ma'am," Patsy said. As she stooped to rub the puppy's back, Mrs. Brubaker disappeared, then returned with a length of rope.

"Tie this around his neck and mind he behaves himself," she said. "Bad manners are not excusable in child nor animal."

"No, ma'am," said Patsy. She made a quick but careful collar around George's neck, took the pouch of shillings Mrs. Brubaker handed her and put it into her skirt pocket, then she led the puppy outside. As she walked toward the street, Mrs. Brubaker called, "There are a few extra shillings in that pouch, Miss Black. If you would like, treat yourself to a candy stick or new handkerchief for your trouble."

Patsy smiled and waved back. "It is no trouble, ma'am, but I thank you for your generosity!" And the puppy and the girl were off onto the busy Philadelphia street.

In spite of the fighting going on with the British in the north beyond the city, Philadelphia still had its charm and pleasantries. Walking along Mulberry's sidewalk, heading east to Mrs. Ross's shop, Patsy observed people going about their afternoon duties. There were citizens and visitors, chatting and moving at brisk paces to and from homes and shops. Women scolded children who lagged behind; men pointed fingers at each other in heated debates on the state of the war and the quality of goods in the city. Several wild dogs trotted side by side and snarled for a moment at George, then went on their way, sniffing about shop doorways for scraps of food.

Patsy's first stop was a shop belonging to Betsy Ross. It was a narrow and sunny three-story house with white-shuttered windows and a fenced side-yard. In the yard, Patsy could see roses and other flowers and a flock of chattering starlings. Patsy tied George to the fence, opened the door and went inside.

Mrs. Ross was a seamstress who had taken over her husband's shop when he died not long ago. She had a good reputation for workmanship; Patsy could tell this the moment she entered the shop. Fine clothes hung about the walls in attractive displays. There was a work table covered with bolts of cloth, spools of thread, scissors and needles.

"Good afternoon, Mrs. Ross," Patsy said to the woman, who had stood up from the table to greet her. "I have an order from Mrs. Josiah Brubaker."

Mrs. Ross wiped her hands free of fabric lint and took the note Patsy held out. "Oh, this will be fine," she said pleasantly. "Tell Mrs. Brubaker I will see if I can find the lace she wants." Mrs. Ross made a *tsk*ing sound. "But I hope she realizes that things are harder to obtain now than ever. It may take a little time. However, I will do my best."

"Thank you," said Patsy. Then she glanced at

the cloth on the table. "What is it you are working on, Mrs. Ross? Is it upholstery for a chair?"

"No, child. I've just begun working on a flag."

"Really? What kind of flag?"

Mrs. Ross only smiled and said, "You are curious, aren't you? Thank you for stopping by. Give Mrs. Brubaker my regards."

Patsy bid Mrs. Ross farewell and left her shop. She collected George, who had tangled himself all up trying to get at the starlings on the other side of the fence, and walked south half a block, down Third Street. Here was the silversmith's shop. There was a tall maple tree beside the shop, and again, Patsy secured the struggling George.

The silversmith's shop sparkled with brightly polished plates and goblets and platters. Mr. Ford, a middle-aged man with hair as silver as his wares, wrapped the tray in brown paper and thanked Patsy for being such a kind neighbor to Mrs. Brubaker.

The third stop would be the apothecary. The shop was on High Street, past the busy central marketplace and Boxler's Milliner. Barbara Layman's mother worked at the milliner's as a clerk. As Patsy and George walked by the shop, Patsy's good friend, Abby Boxler, tapped on the window glass from inside, then skipped outside to the street.

"Patsy Black!" Abby exclaimed. She was a pretty girl with dark hair and brown eyes. She wore a fancy gown of pink and a new bonnet with white and green lace. "I haven't seen you since my mother and I visited the new baby. How is Mrs. Black?"

"She is fine, thank you," Patsy said, working hard to keep George from tugging the end of the rope from her hand. The puppy had spied a mouse scurrying across the cobblestone and was determined to have a chase. "At last she is up and about a bit, checking on things, giving orders like she has always done."

"Wonderful," Abby said. "Your mother was always such a fine lady."

"And your mother?" Patsy asked. "How is Mrs. Boxler?"

Abby's smile faded. She took a deep breath, tugged on the ribbon of her bonnet and glanced over her shoulder at the shop. "Well in health, but not so happy, I'm afraid. In the past months our shop hasn't done well at all. With the war, we no longer receive shipments of the finest materials and clothing from abroad. Nothing comes from England, of course, nor France nor any-where else. Mother has tried to make up for those losses by giving sewing work to several ladies of Philadelphia. These women do excellent work with the cloth they have. Yet linens and woolens are common, and we can't offer specialties now. I fear we may have to sell the business if something doesn't change."

"You mean if the war doesn't end?"

"Yes. I wish that we never went to war. I see troops riding along the street and get very angry. I wish we could get along with the King and noth-ing would change. It's so hard on us. Why can't we just talk things over and end the fighting? If I was a man, I'd go to the State House right now and tell them what I think."

Patsy nodded. She understood Abby's feelings of helplessness. How terrible it would be if the Boxlers lost their business. Mrs. Boxler was a widow, with no one to bring in money but herself. If the shop closed, what would they do? Where would they go?

But Abby brightened, and said, "Enough gloom. How is sweet little Dorcas?"

Patsy said, "She is sweet most of the time. But sometimes she is more irritating than pleasant."

Abby shoved her hands onto her hips. "Oh, Patsy! How can you say such a thing?"

"Easily! You haven't got a baby in your house," Patsy said. "You have no younger brothers or sisters. If you would come and stay with us for a few days, you would understand. I love Dorcas, but I can barely get enough sleep with her waking at all odd hours. And she is so loud! You can't even hear the market bell ringing over her wail when she is hungry. And we wash her clothes nearly all the time. Do you know how fast a baby can soil a gown? We wash and wash and wash. . . ."

Abby, grinning with good humor, threw her hands up to silence her friend. "Enough! I suppose I can't know what it is like. Now, tell me, how did you persuade your mother to let you out of the tavern for a walk?"

"I'm not on a walk, I'm on an errand for my neighbor, Mrs. Brubaker. She is still weak from her spell and her fall. I have been to Mr. Ford's shop, and Mrs. Ross's, and next I visit Dr. Willard's apothecary."

"And you have the puppy with you? I thought he was not to go on any more walks with you. I remember how he caused a man to be thrown from his horse not long ago."

Patsy nodded, then tugged back on the rope as George lunged forward once more. "Yes, but this time I refuse to let the little rascal go. If he goes, I go with him!'"

Abby said, "I must return to help Mother. But wait, I have something for you." She went inside and came out in a moment, carrying a pink rose. She stuck the stem into the rope collar on George's neck. "Now he looks ready to visit the city more properly. A scoundrel dressed up is much more tolerable than a plain scoundrel."

"Thank you!" Patsy said. And off she skipped to the apothecary.

The store was owned by the old doctor, Mr. William Willard. Here, tonics and medicines were sold. Although most treatments for illnesses and injuries were kept at home and women were responsible for tending the sick, there were some items that were too rare or expensive for the normal household. In addition to the medicines the place sold dried foods, candies and soaps. Dr. Willard and his wife both worked at the shop, and the doctor's office, used mostly for setting broken bones and doing amputations, was in back. Until the war, the Willards lived in a house nearby. However, the couple had moved to the apothecary's second floor because of financial difficulties. Special medicines and foods from Europe couldn't get through to Pennsylvania anymore.

Patsy tied George's leash to a horse post outside. The dog looked up at her as if to ask, "Please, I'm so tired of being tied up. Can't I come inside with you?"

But Patsy answered the question he seemed to want to ask. "No, George. You must learn to be good. Now just stay here and watch people go by. I'll be back in a moment. If you behave yourself, I'll find a treat for you when we get back to Mrs. Brubaker's house."

George whined as if he understood, even if it didn't make him much happier.

There was a bell over the door. It tinkled lightly as Patsy came through. Mrs. Willard stood measuring a dark powder into a bottle. She glanced up and smiled at Patsy. "If it isn't little Miss Patsy Black," she said. "How nice to see you. It's been a while since you've been to our shop. And your mother and the precious baby are in fine health, I pray?"

Patsy curtsied quickly. "Yes, ma'am, fine and

well. I'm on an errand for Mrs. Brubaker. She said she sent word yesterday of the items she needed and that they would be ready for me to collect them."

"Indeed, such a good customer she is," Mrs. Willard said. From the crowded wooden shelves behind her, she took several vials and a small corked bottle. "Have you something in which to put these?"

Patsy carefully slipped the items into her pocket. When she moved, however, they clinked together. "Will they break?"

"Perhaps," Mrs. Willard said. She found a piece of clean paper on a lower shelf and wrapped the vials and bottle up, then Patsy put them back into her pocket. She hesitated, looking at the jar of brightly colored candy sticks. Mrs. Brubaker had given her some shillings to spend. Perhaps she could buy one each for herself, Barbara, Henry and Nicholas. They would enjoy them.

"Is there anything else?" Mrs. Willard asked, looking up from the book in which she was inscribing the sale. But the little book reminded Patsy of something she'd rather have. She said, "No, thank you, ma'am," and went outside to get George.

She strolled home the same way she had come, but this time she walked slowly enough to gaze into the shop windows as she passed. George picked up a brisk trot, and Patsy tried to walk fast enough to keep up with him. It was not lady-like to run, and she tried hard to keep from having to. But the puppy was growing stronger every day, it seemed.

And then she passed a bookseller's. Over the door, a brightly painted sign showed a stack of books and a quill pen. This shop belonged to a man named Smith. "Hold up there, George," she said to the dog, but George only tugged several times on the rope, whining and yipping at the shadow of a bird that had caught his attention. "Stop it, now."

In the window of Mr. Smith's shop, behind the wavy glass, Patsy could see a fine and attractive display of books for sale. Patsy herself didn't own any books; they all belonged to her father and to Henry. What if she was to purchase a book of her very own? What a thrill, to own a book! She glanced around, but the posts near the store were occupied by three large horses. She didn't dare tie George up near horses. Either they would stomp him or he would nip at them. And she knew it would not be proper to take a dog into the bookseller's.

"Look at the puppy!" came a child's voice behind Patsy. She glanced back to see a little girl of about six standing with her mother. The mother was chatting with another woman as the child stood twisting her foot in the dirt of the road. "Mother, look at the dog! May I pet the dog? Mother?"

The mother glanced down at her daughter and said, "Would you just stand still for a moment, Polly? I declare that you are as fidgety as a kitten with fleas!" The little girl's shoulders drooped, and she tapped her foot again, stirring up puffs of dust.

Patsy walked over to the girl and the mother. Maybe George would be happier with someone to hold his leash and give him attention this time. "Would it be all right if your daughter kept my dog for a fcw minutes while you are talking? I need to go into the bookseller's for just a moment."

The girl brightened. She hopped up and down and said, "May I hold the dog, Mother? I will be oh-so still if you let me hold the dog!"

The mother seemed glad for there to be a distraction for the little girl, and she said, "Yes, if you will mind yourself."

"Now, hold him firmly but not so tight as to harm him," Patsy said to the child. "Whatever you do, don't let go of this rope. I shall be quick, I promise."

"Do take your time," said the little girl as she knelt down to rub George behind his ears. "I shall keep him safe, I promise." George wagged his tail and licked the girl on the face. The girl giggled.

Patsy went into the bookseller's. The room was cooler than the outdoors, and much darker. It took a moment for her eyes to adjust to the light. When she had focused, she gazed about in wonder.

There were books everywhere, slim volumes and large ones bound in leather. Several men in finely tailored breeches and waistcoats stood talking among shelves, dabbing at their noses with handkerchiefs and pointing their toes in a gentlemanly manner. The shopkeeper—Mr. Smith, Patsy guessed—sat on a stool behind a counter, tallying numbers in a book. He wore a dark wig, which was somewhat askew on his head, and a pair of spectacles. He glanced up at Patsy, and his brows furrowed slightly.

"Young miss, are you lost?" he asked.

"No, sir," Patsy said. "I would care to look about your shop."

The man lay his quill pen aside and stood. "Look about? Are you on an errand for your father, child?"

"No, sir. I would like to purchase a book."

The man smiled, and it made Patsy angry. It was as though he thought she was being silly. "For whom?" he asked.

"For me, sir."

"You have learned to read?"

"Yes, sir. I am not simple-minded."

"How old are you, child?"

Patsy felt anger welling up. Her ears flushed hot and her nose twitched. Who was this man? Not her father nor grandfather! What right had he to question her so? Slowly, she said, "I'm twelve, sir, and I can read as well as many adults. Now, may I have a look at your books or do you mean to toss me out?"

The man's eyes went wide, then he rocked back on his heels in laughter. His wig was shaken so hard with his chuckles that it slid sideways a little bit more. "Certainly then, miss, have a look about the shop. But to save you time, let me recommend a book for you." He lifted a book from the counter. "Foxe's *Book of Martyrs*. Have you read this? It is a holy book you should read as opposed to other trite tales."

"I've not read it," Patsy said. She turned away. She wanted to look herself.

"I've *Aesop's Fables* as well," said the shop-keeper. "And *Robinson Crusoe, Robin Good-Fellow,* and *Mr. Winlove's Collection of Moral Tales.* These would suit your needs."

You don't know my needs, Patsy thought. "I shall look."

The man said nothing more and left her alone.

She browsed undisturbed, finding titles such as *The Plain Man's Pathway to Heaven, Gulliver's Travels,* and *Pilgrim's Progress.* And then, on a table, she discovered several volumes of the book Barbara had: *Common Sense.* Quickly, she snatched one up and took it to the seller. "How much for this one?"

"You should not take that book," said the man. "It is not what little girls are reading. Put that back and have a better look. There is certainly something more appropriate."

"This is the book I want."

One eyebrow raising, he didn't argue anymore. He took Patsy's coins, wrapped the book in brown paper and put it into her hands. "I hope your brother enjoys this. For it is much too complicated for a girl child."

Patsy ignored his comment, took the book outside and unwrapped it so she could see it. She couldn't wait to take the book home. Barbara would no longer have to sneak her father's copy. The Daughters of Liberty would have one to read of their very own.

She skipped over to where the little girl and her mother stood waiting. It was time to take George back to Mrs. Brubaker's house.

But, like Dorcas that morning, George had vanished.

3

"Where is my dog?" Patsy asked. "What happened to George?"

"He was too strong," said the little girl. There were streaks of tears on her face. "He pulled away from me, and my mother wouldn't let me go after."

"Oh, no!" Patsy said. She glanced around, up and down High Street, and could see George nowhere. The puppy had done it again! She knew she shouldn't have taken him for a walk, in spite of what Mrs. Brubaker had said. The puppy was too much of a scoundrel!

"Which way did he run?" Patsy asked. "Quickly!"

The little girl pointed down the street. "There,

and he was running oh-so fast! He was chasing after a horse."

Patsy thought, *George is always after horses! Why can't he learn to stay put?*

Clutching the book with one hand and the silver tray with the other, Patsy ran off in the direction the girl had pointed. Left and right she looked, glancing down narrow alleys, up onto shop steps, behind barrels and pedestrians and horses cinched to posts and railings. She passed clusters of children playing tell-tag and several boys who had scratched a Scotch-Hop grid into a hard-packed plot of roadside and were taking turns tossing a pebble onto the grid.

But George was nowhere to be seen.

"George!" she called. "George, come back here this minute!"

Mrs. Brubaker will be furious if he is lost, she thought with dismay. The woman had trusted Patsy to take good care of him. Patsy had been in trouble with Mrs. Brubaker before, and it was not pleasant. She didn't want to face the woman's temper yet again.

Suddenly there was a barking from nearby. Patsy stopped and squinted in the sun. A tall man stood by his horse, one arm through the reins and one arm around the wiggly body of a black-and-white puppy.

"George!" Patsy cried, hurrying over to the stranger. The man looked up at Patsy and smiled. He had red hair and a pleasant expression. He was well-dressed, and his horse's tack and saddle-bags were of very fine leather, with etched designs along the stitches. This man was not a common man. He was probably rich, indeed.

"Is this little animal your charge?" the man asked. "He was after my horse on the street, nipping and barking at his heels. I dare say if this horse wasn't so well-trained, I would have been off in a flash, trampled beneath hooves and wagon wheels."

Patsy curtsied quickly. Her cheeks were hot with embarrassment. "I apologize, sir. This puppy shall never come out with me again. He has no manners whatsoever."

The stranger scratched George's wiggling chin. "I believe you. And his name is George? I am curious. Is that after King George?"

"No, sir," Patsy said. "My neighbor Mrs. Brubaker named him George after someone else. George Washington, I believe. She says the dog is independent, brave and determined, just like the general."

"George Washington," said the stranger. He tipped his head as if thinking this over. "And do you think the general is independent and brave, as your neighbor does?"

"Sir," Patsy said, but then she bit her tongue to keep from saying more. She was afraid. What if this man was a Tory? What if he was loyal to the king? And she had just told him that her neighbor thought General Washington was brave. "Sir, I have little thought on the matters of the war. I'm only a young girl."

"But I see you read. What volume is that you are carrying?"

Patsy pulled the book behind her back. "It's a surprise for my father, and he is around here close by. I do not want him to see it before we get home."

The stranger nodded, said no more about the book, and put George on the ground. He handed Patsy the end of his rope leash and said in a quiet voice. "Your neighbor sounds like a fine woman. I commend her choice of names."

Patsy felt a little better, although she knew spies could be clever with their comments. She shifted the tray beneath her arm and wrapped the rope's end about her hand tightly so George could not escape.

The man pushed his hat back on his head and said, "I am from out of town, young miss. From the south. I have stayed in several places while here, and I have spent many hours working on a document at the Graff House. However, I have grown restless and am in need of a change for a few days. Can you recommend comfortable lodgings nearby?"

"There is Black's Tavern on Mulberry Street, not far from here. Lodgings are comfortable and the food is the best in the city," said Patsy. "They would welcome you."

"Very well. I thank you." The man bowed, mounted his horse and adjusted his hat. Then he held his hand up in farewell. "Take care of little George. He'll grow up to be a fine dog." With a gentle tap to the horse's sides, the man was off.

"Come, little George," Patsy said as she clutched the book, the tray and the puppy's rope. She touched the pocket of her skirt to make sure in all her haste she hadn't lost Mrs. Brubaker's medicine. "My father will be glad for the extra guest and the extra money. The traveler seems to be one who can pay with ease. But I hope the man isn't a spy. It would be frightening to have a spy in my own home," she confided to the puppy.

George growled at an imaginary cat and tugged on his lead. Patsy turned him around and began her walk home. "But if that man is a spy," she said to the dog and to herself, "then Barbara and I shall find out, and we will tell on him to the members of the Congress. It will be the job of the Daughters of Liberty to let them know all about him!"

4

It was early afternoon. George had been returned to Mrs. Brubaker's house and was presently in her rear garden, barking at birds. Barbara was tending the horses at the stable behind the tavern. Mrs. Black was upstairs, cleaning the guests' rooms. And Patsy was in the family's bedroom with her sleeping baby sister, mending a huge tear in the seat of Nicholas's breeches. Next, she would tackle the holes in her own stockings. The work was slow and tedious; Mother insisted that the stitches be tight and uniform.

"One day you will be doing this for your own children and teaching your daughters to sew," Mother always said. "So do the best you can. The quality of your handiwork reveals the quality of your care for your family."

Patsy held the breeches up and checked the stitches. They looked flawless. She had promised herself that her mother would find the work perfect. After such a hectic morning, losing Dorcas and then losing the puppy George, Patsy was glad to be safe in the bedroom, working on mending breeches.

Dorcas was silent in her sleep. Every few minutes, Patsy glanced over and smiled. When Dorcas was four, Patsy would help her learn to write and to use a needle, too. That would be fun. She'd tried to teach Barbara such skills, but Barbara never was interested.

Suddenly there was a shout from outside the window. Patsy hopped up and strained to see what was going on, but could see very little beyond the side garden. The shout came again. It was a man's voice.

"Help! Water! My shop's on fire!"

The breeches slid from Patsy's hands and onto the floor. Fire? There was a fire behind the tavern? The only shop on tavern property was the blacksmith shop, belonging to Mr. Norris.

Patsy could see smoke rising up above the

branches of the oak and maple trees of the side garden. Yes, it was Mr. Norris's shop. She should help! He would need all the hands he could get to fill buckets from the well and put out the blaze.

But I can't leave Dorcas alone. Not again. Not even to stop the fire!

"What should I do?" she said aloud, a sob escaping with the words. "This is terrible. Mr. Norris can't lose his shop, it is all he has!"

But as if her mother had heard her, Mrs. Black rushed into the room, shouting, "Patsy, I cannot help in my condition, but go quickly to the back and assist your brother. The blacksmith's shop is burning! Run now, quickly!"

In a flash, Patsy was out of the room, down the hall, and into the backyard. The smell of smoke was strong outside, and a column of smoke could be seen rising in the air over the kitchen and the tavern's small grove of apple trees.

The Anderson sisters, twin Quaker ladies who helped with the chores at the tavern, stood side by side, staring at the smoke with wide eyes, like those of frightened squirrels. They held wooden poles with which they had been stirring laundry in the large cooking pot.

"Drop those and follow me!" Patsy said as she

raced past them. "Laundry can wait. Mr. Norris is losing his shop!"

The ladies hesitated, then in unison the poles fell to the grass, and they were after Patsy as quickly as their prim legs could carry them.

The tavern well was behind the kitchen, and already Mr. Layman, Mr. Norris, Mr. Norris's young apprentice, Randolph Bonner, and Patsy's older brother, Henry, were filling oak buckets and racing them past the apple trees and smokehouse to the small blacksmith's shop near the stable. Smoke and flames poured from the windows and door of the blacksmith's shop. The outer walls were charred and black. Patsy's heart clenched in fear. Mr. Norris would lose his life's work if they didn't stop the fire. And the fire could quickly turn with a breeze, sending it to the stable, where the horses were bedded!

Henry saw Patsy first and waved at her anxiously. "We need more buckets," he called as he drew up the newly filled well's bucket from the depths, poured the water into the one held by Mr. Layman and then lowered it back for more. Mr. Layman ran the water to the shop and tossed it through one window. "Get some buckets from the stable and make haste!" Henry shouted.

Patsy ran to the paddock, climbed over the gate and went into the stable. The Anderson ladies, unwilling to climb, took an extra moment and opened the gate to pass through.

"Barb!" Patsy shouted for her friend. "Barb, where are you? We need you! Come help us!"

She slid to a stop in front of the stall of Barbara's pony, Little Bit. It was empty. Barbara was out riding somewhere. Patsy slammed the stall door open and grabbed Little Bit's half-filled bucket, sloshing water all over her arms. Horses in the other stalls whinnied and snorted and stomped, nervous at the smell of smoke in the nearby building. The Anderson ladies stood inside the stable, confused and nervous. Patsy shouted, "Buckets in the stalls! Don't just stand there. Hurry!"

The ladies followed suit, clutching the hems of their skirts so as not to trip. Less than a minute later, all three were running with wooden buckets to the well for Henry to fill.

"It's burning too fast!" Mr. Norris shouted as he threw another bucketful of water through the shop door onto the blaze. "We aren't slowing it. I'm going to lose my shop. God help me, I'm going to lose everything!"

Patsy held her bucket as Henry filled it. Then as quickly as she could, she ran to the shop. Smoke was hanging low, and she coughed and squinted, trying to see well enough to pour the water through the window. But as she lifted the bucket, the weight of the water shifted and it all poured out onto the ground.

"No!" she shouted. *I've wasted water, I've wasted time!*

Beside her, Randolph tossed water at the flame, then grabbed her by the shoulder. "Don't dawdle! Come on! Barbara's gone for help, but we must keep fighting it!" They went back to the well, refilled the buckets and returned. This time, Patsy steadied her hand and the water went onto the flames.

One Anderson sister tossed water into the shop, then the other. For what seemed like a long time, Patsy and the others ran back and forth with sloshing buckets, dodging each other, coughing through the smoke, the skin on their arms and faces singeing with the extreme heat. But the fire grew, its glowing fingers reaching higher and wider, not slowed at all by the steady dousing.

And then Henry shouted, "Barbara's here!"

Little Bit galloped onto the tavern property,

and Barbara pulled her to a stop by the paddock fence. Behind Barbara came a horseless wagon with steel wheels, side handles and a leather hose with a long brass nozzle. Four men ran alongside of the wagon, steering it with the handles. It was a fire brigade.

"Thank God!" Mr. Norris cried. "It might not be too late to save my shop!"

Immediately two men dragged the hose from the wagon, stretching it straight and pointing the brass nozzle at the fiery building. Henry, Randolph and Mr. Layman continued to throw water onto the flames as Mr. Norris ran to help work the fire wagon's pump. With grunts and shouts, the men pushed into the pump, and water was forced from the nozzle. Patsy could hear a sizzling sound as the water hit the flame. Barbara slid from Little Bit's saddle, tied the reins to the fence railing, grabbed up Mr. Norris's bucket, and ran with it to the well.

Patsy carried her filled bucket to the shop and tossed it at the fire. Her lungs burned with the soot she had breathed. Her eyes stung mightily. But she couldn't stop yet.

Then Mr. Norris shouted, "It's not working. That's enough for the building. Pour the water on the grass about the shop. Drench the hedges and the ground nearby! We shan't save my shop, but we must keep the fire from spreading to the stable or to Mrs. Brubaker's yard!"

"No!" Henry called from the well. "We won't give up your shop so easily!"

Mr. Norris pushed a man away from the hose and took it firmly in his hands. He directed the nozzle at the ground in front of the shop. Water sprayed the grass.

"Mr. Norris!" Henry shouted. "Don't give up yet!"

But Mr. Norris was defiant on this. His expression was stony, his cheeks streaked with ash. "It's gone. Do what I say, Henry!"

Reluctantly, the men with the buckets poured their water all around the shop, soaking the ground, the bushes nearby and the fencing around the smokehouse and the paddock. Barbara and Patsy, without speaking to each other, did the same. The walls of the blacksmith's shop trembled and then collapsed inward. The fire leaped up and then began to grow smaller.

"It's burning itself out," Henry said, coming up to Patsy and putting his arm around his little sister's shoulder. "It won't go any farther than this."

"Poor Mr. Norris," Barbara said. "He's lost his shop."

"Such a shame," Patsy said.

"Such a pity!" came a voice Patsy didn't recognize. She looked behind her. There, with a frown of concern on his face and the fine leather saddlebags over his shoulder, was the tall stranger who had caught the puppy for her earlier that day, the red-haired man who had asked her about a place to stay. "What a loss. How could this have happened?"

"Sir," Mr. Norris said to the stranger, "I believe there may have been an accident inside my shop. Sparks on ill-placed rags may well have been my downfall. I was out for an hour, and my apprentice was to mind the shop. However, he left to speak with his brother, and I fear the door was left open, letting a wind blow through."

Randolph dropped his head and said, "It was only a moment I was gone. My brother came to show me a new mare, and I only gazed at her for a minute or two, just at the stable gate not fifty feet from the shop! The fire came up so quickly. What am I to do?"

"I do not know," Mr. Norris said.

"How can I ever repay you?"

His words trembling with emotion, Mr. Norris said, "Randolph, I cannot think of it now. We'll talk later."

As Henry, Mr. Norris and the stranger talked about the dreadful loss, and as Randolph and Mr. Layman poured more buckets of well water onto the smoldering remains of the blacksmith's shop, Patsy pulled Barbara aside.

"That tall man," Patsy said, "I met him this morning as I was doing errands for Mrs. Brubaker. George had gotten away again, and this man gave him back to me. Do you think there is something suspicious about him?"

"Such as what?"

"He had a lot of questions for me, asking me what book I had hid behind my back."

"What book did you have?"

"I bought a copy of *Common Sense* for the Daughters of Liberty."

"Oh!" Barbara said. "That's wonderful."

"But the man," Patsy continued, her voice shaking slightly, "he asked me about my thoughts on George Washington! He talked as if he were a British spy."

"Really?" Barbara's eyebrows went up. "A

spy! Oh, Patsy, how exciting. Do you think he started the fire?"

"Perhaps. He only just now appeared, and not in time to help put it out."

"He *must* be a spy," said Barbara. "He followed you home without a reason."

Patsy hesitated, then said, "But he did ask if I could recommend lodging, as he was in need of new surroundings. I told him about our place."

"Then he has an honest reason to be here?"

"I suppose," Patsy said. "But he still might be a spy. How would we know?"

Barbara rubbed her chin solemnly. "We can't know yet. But we must watch him carefully. Report to me anything he says or does that is suspicious."

"Barbara!" Mr. Layman called. "We've done what we can here. We have it under control. Put Little Bit into her stall and then get on your duties. The guests' horses need their grain and water, and an extra grooming to steady them after the fright of the fire. Make haste, daughter."

Barbara said, "Keep your eye on the stranger, Patsy." Then she hurried off to the stable to do her chores.

Patsy collected the buckets, returned them to

the stable, then headed back to the tavern along the dirt path. But something caught her eye, a piece of tattered and scorched paper snagged in the leaves of a boxwood hedge not far from the ruins of the blacksmith's shop. She tugged the paper free, and as she read it, her eyes grew wide.

"This is what happens to smiths who will not support the King's efforts against ruthless traitors! Take much care, Roger Norris!"

The note was left for Mr. Norris! The fire was not an accident; it had been started by someone loyal to the Crown who was angry that Mr. Norris had refused to use his skills to help the Redcoats.

Patsy turned back toward the gathering of men. Mr. Norris was surrounded, talking urgently to Henry, Randolph, Mr. Layman and a constable who had just arrived. But then Henry looked up at Patsy and said, "Get inside now, Patsy. This discussion is for men, not for a young girl. Go."

Well! Patsy thought. *I have the note, so it is for young girls after all. The Daughters of Liberty will find out what this means.* Into her pocket went the note, to show Barbara as soon as they were back together again.

As Patsy passed the small brick kitchen, which was in the backyard, separate from the tavern,

Katherine called from the door, "The fire's out now?"

"Yes," Patsy said. "It will not spread farther. But the shop is destroyed."

Katherine wiped her hands on her apron and nodded. "Then come here. I need you to work the churn. I've got fresh breads baking and we need fresh butter. Come on now, churning will take your mind off the troubles of this afternoon."

Patsy sighed and nodded. She helped Katherine move the churn outside the kitchen into the grass of the yard. There Patsy could sit on a wooden bench and enjoy occasional breezes as she moved the paddle up and down in the milk.

To help pass the time and to keep her mind off the fire, she repeated a rhyme she'd learned as a little girl.

"Two bonnie blackbirds sitting on a hill.
One named Jack and one named Jill.
Fly away Jack, fly away Jill.
Come back Jack, come back Jill."

If I were a boy like Nicholas, she thought, *I would take off my shoes and stockings and feel the green grass beneath my toes.* But young ladies had to remain in a formal state of dress. Anything less would be unheard of and most inappropriate. Toes had to stay hidden.

As hard as she tried to keep from doing so, she couldn't stop thinking about the fire and wondering over and over again who had started it. She thought of the note tucked away in her pocket. *Who wrote it? Is it someone I know? Is it the stranger with the nice saddlebags?*

Patsy began to pound the paddle to the rhythm of the warning.

> "This is what happens,
> to smiths who will not,
> support the King's efforts,
> against ruthless traitors!"

The whole thing made Patsy's head begin to ache dreadfully. But her mind wouldn't let it go.

A half hour later, Katherine called from the kitchen door, "Are you hungry?"

It was nearing three-thirty, and Patsy had heard her stomach rumble a few times. "Yes!" she said.

"I made something for dinner, but I just happen to have a slice or two too many. Would you help me get rid of them?"

Whatever it was, Patsy was willing. Katherine came over to Patsy's stool and handed her a slice of fresh warm cornbread with a small touch of melting butter on a linen towel. Katherine stood beside her and ate her slice as Patsy let go of the paddle and, trying not to show bad manners by eating too quickly, took small bites, savoring the taste.

When done, she dabbed her mouth with the towel and handed it back to Katherine, who patted Patsy's mobcap and said, "Check the butter, and if it is done, bring the churn inside. The men in the Ulysses Room will be pleased to have enough for their dining."

Patsy lifted the lid and saw the butter was thickening and nearly done, with only a puddle of liquid standing at the bottom. She worked a few more minutes with the paddle, then carefully carried the heavy churn back to the kitchen. At the large table the Anderson sisters were helping Katherine put the last of the prepared meats, vegetables, fruits and soup onto large platters and into bowls to be taken to the guests at the tavern.

The ladies lifted the larger plates and Patsy took two smaller ones, and the three of them marched across the yard to the tavern.

Inside, men were settling down, talking heartily among themselves, tucking large white serviettes into their collars so as not to soil their clothing with spilled drink or food. Henry and Nicholas were already serving ale in mugs as quickly as possible without spilling any. Mrs. Black was in the pantry, peering out at the diners. Little Dorcas was in a blanket-lined basket on the counter, deep in sleep. Mrs. Black said to Patsy and the women when they entered, "We've more today than I would have expected, and a hungry lot they are. Be alert and courteous as always and our fine reputation will continue."

"Yes, ma'am," Patsy, Katherine and the Anderson sisters said, almost at the same time.

Patsy carried salt cellars, butter and bread to the tables while Kathcrine and the Anderson sisters brought the first course of turtle soup, ladling a good portion to each man. Patsy had served many, many guests over the years, but the redhaired stranger seated by the far window had her attention more than any she could ever remember. He chatted casually with the three men who shared his table, but his gaze continued to wander to the window, as if he really wasn't listening to his companions.

"Good afternoon, sir," Patsy said to the man as she reached his table with bread and butter. "I hope you find Black's Tavern to your liking."

The man nodded. "You are employed here?"

"My father owns this place. I am Patsy Black."

"It's a pleasure to meet you formally," said the man. "And my name is . . ." But suddenly something outside caught the stranger's eye, and he leaped from his chair, nearly tipping it over backward. He dashed from the Ulysses Room and out into the hall. Patsy could hear the front tavern door slam shut.

"Such energy on such a terribly hot day," said one man at the table. He and another looked at each other with bemused smiles, then went about their business of breaking bread and slathering the pieces with butter.

But all Patsy could think was *Only a man who is a spy would behave so oddly! I must watch out for him. He is a danger, to be certain, and he is here, staying in our tavern!*

5

The clock on the mantel read five past seven. The sun was still shining, but it was low, hiding behind Philadelphia's buildings and trees to the west. The men had finished their meal two hours ago, and they had gone out on evening strolls or had retired to the Red Horse Room for games or to their bed chambers to read.

Patsy had helped her mother change Dorcas's clout and clothes and put the baby to bed in the cradle. Now Patsy had a few free minutes to spend with Barbara at the stable. Patsy had told her mother she was going to give Barbara a reading lesson, and this was the truth. Only she hadn't told her mother the reading material would be the note she'd found in the brush near the burned-down blacksmith's shop.

The girls were in an empty stall at the back of the stable. One visitor had taken his horse down to the river, saying he would be back later. Barbara had picked out the few clumps of manure and thrown down handfuls of fresh straw, making a comfortable seat. However, even though Barbara sat down, Patsy chose to lean against the grain trough. She didn't want scratchy straw in her stockings.

"I must show you what I found!" Patsy said in a hushed voice, holding the note in her hands but not opening it yet. "I know now the fire at the shop was not an accident."

Barbara grinned as if Patsy were teasing, but her smile faded when she saw Patsy's lips stay tight. "Why do you say that?"

"I found a note. Here it is." She unfolded it, smoothed it out and showed it to her friend. "It was near the shop, caught up in a bush as if the breeze from the fire had blown it there. Mr. Norris was supposed to find it. Can you read any of it?"

Barbara squinted at the paper. She said, "It's about the King?"

Patsy said, "Listen. 'This is what happens to smiths who will not support the King's efforts against ruthless traitors. Take much care, Roger Norris!'"

Barbara's mouth fell open. She jumped up, peered over the stall door, out the window, then dropped back to the straw. "Oh, Patsy! This is serious. As Daughters of Liberty, we must do something about this."

"I thought so, too. But I don't know what. Perhaps we should show my father right away and have him take care of it."

Barbara shook her head. "Not yet, please! Give us a day to see what we can find. Our fathers are busy with their duties, are they not? If we could find out who wrote this note and then let our fathers know, we will not only save them the trouble, but we will be known as true and brave patriots!"

"So you say that not telling them right away is doing them a favor?"

Barbara nodded vigorously.

Patsy couldn't help but giggle. Then the seriousness of the matter came back. "If we decide not to share the note, we must not take more than a day to see if we can discover the truth about the stranger. I think he may indeed have something to do with the fire. Do you have any ideas?"

"His handwriting," Barbara said. "Sneak into his bedchamber and see if he has a journal. Most men keep journals. My father does."

"As does mine," Patsy said.

"Take the man's journal and match the writing with the note. This way, we'll know if we have our culprit."

"That is a wonderful plan," Patsy said. "But I am forbidden to go upstairs after dinner, as the men require their privacy."

"Can you send Henry?"

"He would tell Father immediately about the scheme."

"And what about Nicholas? He's only seven and likes secret tricks. We could convince him to steal about and be quiet about it for a candy stick, could we not?"

Patsy pondered this. Nicholas loved candy. She knew he would do just about anything for something sweet to eat. He wouldn't care that Patsy wanted him to sneak a gentleman's journal from his bedchamber. All he would want to know was how soon he could get his reward.

"Yes," she said at last. "I'll send Nicholas on a little spy mission for the Daughters of Liberty. We'll know soon enough if the stranger set the fire."

"You best let me know as soon as you find out," Barbara said. "And together we can present the evidence to your father."

The girls clasped hands to seal the secret and the plan, then Patsy hurried back to the tavern. Mrs. Black spied her passing down the hall.

"Patsy, Katherine is with Dorcas now. It is time for her to do other chores. I want you to stay with your sister until the family retires for the evening."

"But it isn't yet eight o'clock."

"I can read a clock as well as you, daughter. Do as I say."

How will I find Nicholas and have him go upstairs if I have to sit with the baby? she thought. But she curtsied and said to her mother, "Very well." And then, grumbling quietly enough that her mother wouldn't hear, she went to the bedroom. Katherine was sitting in the chair, tending Dorcas. Katherine bid Patsy a good evening and left. Patsy sat on the chair and watched as Dorcas tossed in her sleep.

"We might have a spy upstairs," Patsy whispered to her sister. "But don't be alarmed. Daughters of Liberty will find out for certain."

It looked as if Dorcas smiled.

Well, Patsy thought after several long, boring minutes. *I can read my copy of* Common Sense. *That is better than sitting like a log.*

The book was hidden beneath the pillow of her trundle bed. Patsy had felt sneaky hiding it there, but she didn't think her father would approve of her owning such a book. Andrew Black hated the war, although he hated the tyranny of King George, too. Unfair taxes had made it difficult for almost everyone in the colonies. Mr. Black had been a Son of Liberty in Philadelphia several years ago, until his best friend was caught as a spy by the British and hanged. Since then, Father didn't like to hear any discussion on the matter. It made him angry. It made him sad.

"But he has told us we have to make up our own minds about the war," Patsy said quietly to herself. "Dorcas, tell me what you think?"

Dorcas's eyelids fluttered in a baby's dream, but she remained silent.

"I'm glad you agree with me," Patsy said. She opened the slim volume. It began:

" 'Some writers have so confounded society with government, as to leave little or no distinction between them; whereas they are not only different but have different origins.' "

Patsy took a deep breath. She didn't understand what Mr. Paine was saying in this section any better than she did when she'd read the line to Barbara. She skimmed down a bit farther.

" 'Society in every state is a blessing, but Government, even in its best state, is but a necessary evil; in its worst state an intolerable one.' "

This made a little more sense. A government was necessary for people, but that didn't mean it was always good. A government was like parents. They were necessary, but not always good. Patsy knew a boy named Benjamin who had lived with his father in the rooms above the Black's Tavern stable before the Laymans came. The man was cruel to his son; he beat the boy for no reason. At last, the boy stood up to his father and the two got into a dreadful fight. The father was nearly killed, but he recovered and agreed to never strike his son again. If only the King would agree to leave the colonies alone, they wouldn't have to fight each other.

Patsy jumped to another page. Here, Mr. Paine

said that neither nature nor the scriptures gave any man the right to take total control over others. Such strong statements! It felt uncomfortable to read, even though something inside Patsy made her want to continue. After all, she hated injustice, as did Mr. Paine and many others in Philadelphia. And then she read, " 'The last cord is broken . . . everything that is right or reasonable pleads for separation.' "

"Mr. Paine doesn't think there is hope for peace unless we are free from the Crown," Patsy said to Dorcas. "What will life be like for you, my sister? Will you live as an independent American or grow up as a British citizen?"

"What are you reading, Patsy?"

Patsy almost jumped out of her chair. Slamming the book shut in her lap, she looked up to see Nicholas standing in the doorway. It looked as if he'd fallen in a rain barrel. His clothes were soaked. Water had flattened his hair to his head, and a drop clung to the tip of his nose.

"Why, nothing," she answered. She put the book facedown on the small table beside her. "And what has happened to you?"

Nicholas dropped his soaked hat onto the floor, then peeled off his vest. "I got into a fight!" he said, grinning ear to ear. "With Richard Cannon. Henry and I were down at the river, selecting shellfish from the boats. Richard was there with his father. We got to talking about the war, and Richard didn't like what I said."

"What did you say?"

"That we had no choice but to defend ourselves from the British. Then Richard said we *were* British! Hah! What an imbecile. So I pushed him and he pushed me. We both went in. But he had to be dragged out, screaming and crying. I swim better than he does!"

"Oh," Patsy said. "You'll not find that everyone agrees with you, Nicholas. I'm afraid you often have to watch your words or you might well find yourself in your own little war. Did Henry let you come inside like that?"

"Like what?" Nicholas looked down at himself. His eyes widened as if for the first time he realized how wet he was. "Oh!"

"You are making a dreadful mess," Patsy continued. "You need to go out back to the kitchen. Katherine will dry your clothes and you won't spoil our floor."

Nicholas scowled, but Patsy picked up his ruined hat and gave it back to him. "Out of here, now," she said. "Get to the kitchen."

His leather shoes squeaking with the water, Nicholas turned to leave the bedroom. But then Patsy remembered her talk with Barbara and jumped up.

"Wait!" she called softly. "Before you go, I have a request."

Nicholas frowned. "No, Patsy. I won't sit with the baby. I'm not a girl!"

"That isn't what I want," Patsy said. "It's a request that is actually quite dangerous. Are you interested in adventure?"

Nicholas scowled. "I don't know."

"For a stick of candy?"

Nicholas's face brightened. "I should think I might."

Patsy said, "There is a man staying here in the tavern. He is tall, with red hair. I need you to do something, but you must be very careful. He may be a British spy."

Nicholas was instantly curious. He listened carefully as Patsy told him of her plan. And he promised that as soon as he was in dry clothes, he would do as she asked.

Patsy then sent him off to the kitchen. When

she sat back down in the chair beside Dorcas's cradle, she realized that she was shaking in her shoes.

"We'll know soon enough," she told the sleeping baby. "And if we have a spy, we'll have him captured and jailed so he'll never be a danger to freedom-loving Patriots again!"

6

Patsy listened with her head tilted to the side, wondering if the footsteps she heard upstairs were Nicholas's or someone else's.

He's been gone for over twenty minutes! she thought.

It was growing dark outside and soon Patsy would have to light the candles in the bedroom. Surely Nicholas had had time to change his wet clothes and go up to peek through the stranger's belongings for a note or journal with his handwriting.

"He's so slow," Patsy complained to her baby sister. "What is keeping him? I told him what the stranger's saddlebags looked like. A look inside for a journal or a note is all we need to prove the man is a spy!"

Dorcas wiggled and sighed softly.

"Soon Mother will be in to feed you," Patsy said. "Then I can go out to the hall." She shook her head. "But what good will that do? If I call out for Nicholas, that will bring attention to my plan. And I can't go upstairs to see what is keeping him so long. I'm a girl, and a girl is forbidden there this time of evening."

But a boy isn't forbidden, Patsy thought suddenly. She put her hand to her mouth in surprise at the plan that had jumped into her mind. She could borrow some of Henry's clothes and go upstairs, disguised as a boy! If she was careful, no one would know who she was. She could find out what had detained her little brother.

Her heart beating madly, Patsy opened the wardrobe and found a pair of breeches, a hat, a shirt and a waistcoat. They would be large, but it was the best she could do.

"But I can't leave this room in Henry's clothes," she said to herself. "Everyone would see and know it was me."

Then she heard her mother's voice in the room beyond the door, speaking to someone in the Red

Horse Room. Mrs. Black was coming to feed Dorcas. Without another thought, Patsy tossed Henry's clothes out the window to the garden. The door opened.

"Hello, daughter!" Mrs. Black said, softly yet cheerfully. "I see you and Dorcas are having a nice evening."

"Yes, ma'am," Patsy said. She wondered if the clothes had tangled on the rose bush below the window. Would her mother see them hanging there? She moved in front of the window, blocking the view.

"It is getting late," Mrs. Black said. "The sun is going down. Your father, Henry and Nicholas will be in soon, and it will be time for scripture, for our family prayers, and then bed. I suppose you are as glad as I to have a good night's sleep!"

"Yes, ma'am," Patsy said. *But I have to find out what happened to Nicholas. I have to find out about the stranger!*

Mrs. Black picked up the baby and held her closely. Patsy watched, making herself smile, trying to think of a way to get out for just a few minutes.

"Mother," she said. "I left my dolls, Sallie Jones and Mrs. Byrd, down at the stable. I think they are in a stall where Barbara and I visited earlier. Please, may I go find them and bring them back? I'm afraid if they stay there all night, a horse might find them and take a bite out of them."

"How careless!"

"Yes, I know. I'm sorry. Please, may I go?"

"Hmmm," said Mrs. Black. "I suppose. Those dolls are too nice to leave in a stall. But make sure you shake the straw off them before you bring them inside."

"Yes, ma'am, and thank you!" Patsy said. And she was out of the room before her mother could tell her how soon to be back.

Patsy crept around the back of the tavern and through the gate, easing it closed so it wouldn't make a clapping noise. In the side garden, she could see through the window that her mother had already lit two candles over the fireplace. Patsy hastily gathered Henry's clothes, which had fallen clear of the rose bushes and were in a heap on the grass. Stepping between a maple tree and Mrs. Brubaker's brick wall, Patsy slipped into the trousers and out of her mobcap, dress and petticoats. The shirt went on over her head and was tucked into the trousers. The waistcoat and hat finished the outfit. She knew it might seem strange to be wearing girls' shoes, but with luck, no one would notice. Her own clothes were folded and placed behind the tree. She was surprised at how comfortable Henry's clothes were. No petticoats or stays or bulky skirts.

Now, she thought, *all I have to do is hurry upstairs before anyone notices me.* She went out the garden's front gate and walked to the tavern's entrance. The street lamp had been lit. It cast an orange glow that blended with the last golden sparkles of daylight. There were still travelers on the street, but not so much as earlier. The air was, at last, cooling.

A man met Patsy as he came out of the tavern door. He said, "Good evening, boy."

Patsy pulled the hat down to cover her eyes and said in her deepest voice, "Good evening, sir."

This is something Barbara would do, she thought nervously as she stepped into the foyer. *My throat is so dry I can barely swallow!*

Without looking left or right, Patsy grabbed the banister and rushed up the steps. No one had seen her downstairs. Next, she only had to find Nicholas and see if he'd discovered a journal.

To the right were three bedchambers. On tiptoe, Patsy went to the open doorway of the first. There were two beds with hangings still tied to the bedposts. Candles on a small round table had been lit. One gentleman smoked a pipe and stared out of the window, his back to the door. He was not the stranger. And she did not see the saddlebags.

Patsy went to the second room. This one had three beds, and no men were inside. And again, the saddlebags were not there.

The door to the last room was partially shut. As Patsy stepped to it, she could hear the voices inside—several men and a boy.

Nicholas! What is he doing, visiting? He is supposed to be snooping for the Daughters of Liberty!

Inching closer, she leaned over and looked through the doorway. Inside, around a table, were three men and Nicholas, playing cards and laughing. Nicholas was even smoking a pipe! If Mother had seen this, she would have been furious. But Patsy was furious for another reason. Nicholas had forgotten why Patsy sent him upstairs.

He has lost a candy stick, then. That is his own decision. I should have known better than to expect him to complete a task for me. And I can't even tell on him. He is upstairs because I asked him to come.

None of the men playing cards with Nicholas was the stranger. Patsy backed away and walked down the hall to the other bedchambers.

How long have I been gone? Patsy wondered as she moved to the bedchamber left of the stairs. *Only five minutes or so, I hope. I must do this quickly before Mother begins to worry that I've gotten myself lost.*

"But this is for independence," she said to herself in a whisper. "This is for freedom and the Patriots." Her arms were shaking. The blood in her veins felt cold.

The first room had a single man, already asleep on one of the beds. He snored so harshly that the drapes on the posts wavered with each breath. No saddlebags could be seen

Maybe he's got them with him. Maybe he's hidden them beneath a bed or pillow so a fellow guest won't riffle through them like I plan on doing.

She stopped in front of the open door to the second room. No man was there, but draped across the back of a chair near the fireplace were the saddlebags. She knew they were his when she spotted the fine expensive leather and the etched designs.

"Quickly," she said to herself. "He will surely have something with his handwriting in those saddlebags. Take it and get downstairs right away!"

There were footsteps coming up the stairs. Patsy turned and pretended to be gazing out the dormer windows to the backyard. A man went by her and walked to the last chamber on the left. She glanced at him as he passed. He was a short old man with a potbelly and spectacles—not the stranger. She let out a sigh of relief.

Patsy slipped into the second bedchamber. With trembling hands, she lifted the saddlebags, slipped open the buckles on one side and looked inside. It was empty. She opened the second side. This pocket had only several newspapers, folded neatly.

This isn't going to be easy at all. This wasn't a good idea! What was I thinking?

On the table by the chair was a coat, hat and small leather case. A well of ink and pen lay beside them. Did these belong to the stranger, too? Patsy looked at the door and paused, listening. There was no one in the hall. She looked back at the case. She took a deep breath and, with trembling fingers, unlocked the case and lifted the lid.

Inside was only a violin.

"Are you a lover of music as well as a lover of books?" came a loud voice from the doorway.

Patsy jumped back, the lid falling closed and her hat flying from her head. She spun around. There, with hands on his hips, was the tall stranger. He wasn't smiling this time. His eyebrows were pulled together into a serious unhappy line.

"I," Patsy began. Her tongue refused to work. What could she say?

The stranger came into the room. "Am I to suppose that your puppy got away from you again and you followed him up here? That he might have found himself a hiding place in my violin case?"

Patsy shook her head. No words would come. She had been caught trespassing in this man's room as well as looking through his belongings. *Will they put me in the stocks down near the marketplace? Oh, no! I am done for!*

The stranger went to the table and snapped the violin case shut. He said nothing for a moment, but he looked at the floor and then the ceiling.

But he's a spy, Patsy thought. *If I can prove*

it, then it won't be me arrested but him. I must stand strong.

"What are you searching for, child?" the stranger said finally. The gaze of his eyes was so intense that it made Patsy shiver.

"Just looking, sir," she said at last.

"Do you think I have something of value? Something you might steal and sell?"

"Oh, no! I am not a thief! I am Patsy Black, daughter of Andrew and Rebecca Black!"

"Then if you are not a thief, you are a spy?"

"A spy! No sir! I am only a girl who helps her family with the care of this tavern."

"And dressed as a boy? I don't know many girls who play in boy's clothes. A disguise is the sign of a spy. Are you here on behalf of the King?"

"No, sir!"

"They hang spies, you know."

"Yes, sir, I know! I'm not a spy!"

The man nodded slowly. Then he said, "Then tell me the truth. What are you here for?"

Can I tell the truth? Can I betray the Daughters of Liberty? Am I as brave as the soldiers who could give their life for the cause of independence? Tears sprang into Patsy's eyes. She dug them away with her fist. Then she said, "My brother and I are playing a game. He bet I could not come upstairs and take a small token without being found out a girl."

"Your shoes," said the stranger.

"Yes, I know," Patsy said.

"And the token?"

"Oh, just something worthless. An old scrap of paper, I thought."

The stranger shook his head, but his expression softened a little. "Childish games can often get someone into serious trouble."

"Yes, sir."

"But you want to win this bet with your brother. You want a token, and you want to not be seen as a girl."

I really want to see if your handwriting matches the note I found near the burned blacksmith's shop, Patsy thought. But she said, "Yes, sir."

The man lifted the violin case from the table. Beneath it was a small stack of writing paper. The top sheet had been written on. It looked like a letter.

"I have some newspapers somewhere," said the stranger. "I thought they were here."

Patsy had to bite her lip to keep from saying they were in the saddlebags. She didn't want him to know how much sneaking she had done. As the man looked around the room, Patsy leaned over and studied the letter.

It read, *"My dearest Martha, I cannot tell you how the heat in Philadelphia makes me long for my home in Virginia . . ."*

The handwriting was not the same as the note to Roger Norris.

"Ah, here," said the stranger. He had found the paper in the saddlebags. "A copy of the *Virginia Gazette.* Take it to your brother, and if you are so inclined to look inside, there is a poem you might enjoy."

"Thank you, sir."

"I admire your courage, if not your choice of games."

Patsy took the paper and curtsied. It felt strange to do so in trousers. She turned to leave the room, but the man said, "You took me as a spy, did you not? In truth, you came up here to see if you could find something to prove your suspicions."

Patsy's mouth fell open.

"I know your father is a good man, and he has sympathies with the Patriots. It wouldn't be strange to assume you shared those sympathies.

I've noticed you staring at me as if you thought I had two heads. What made you afraid of me?"

Patsy blurted out, "The way you talk."

"I am from Virginia. My tone is different from those of Pennsylvanians."

"The way you act."

"Act?"

"You ran out of dinner so abruptly. Who would do so except a nervous spy?"

With this, the man threw back his head and laughed loud and long. Patsy felt her ears flush red with anger. What was so funny? He *had* acted suspiciously!

The man said, "I had left my violin at the other tavern. I saw the hired boy bringing it along the street to me, tossing the case up and down. I couldn't bear the thought of him dropping it. Of course I had to run out!"

"Oh," Patsy said.

Still smiling, the man said, "Do you still take me for a British spy?"

"No," Patsy said.

"Good, then. Go on down with your token and reap your reward."

Patsy curtsied again and then bolted downstairs and out the front door. In the side garden, she quickly slipped back into her own clothing as her father, in the family's bedroom, said, "And where is Patsy, Nicholas? It's time for scriptures."

"I don't know, Father," came Nicholas's voice. "I am always where I'm supposed to be. She should be just like me!"

Then Mr. Black added, "Nicholas, do I smell smoke all over you? What is this?"

"Oh, sir," Nicholas said. "I was upstairs bringing a fresh towel to a gentleman. He accidentally dumped the bowl of his pipe all over me, and I had to brush my hair hard to get the ash all out."

"Mmmm," Mr. Black said.

Patsy groaned. *I have to move quickly!* She threw Henry's clothes over her arm and hurried them to the kitchen. If Henry looked for them tomorrow, she would say they'd gone out for laundering. She folded the newspaper twice more and put it into her skirt pocket, then went to join her family.

Do I still take him for a British spy? she asked herself as she sat on the bed beside her mother and her father opened the family Bible to the flickering light of a lantern. *I don't think so.*

But I can't be certain until I'm certain!

7

Patsy sat on the wooden bench with a bowl in her lap and a bowl at her feet in the grass, snapping beans in the tavern's backyard. Mrs. Layman had grown a large crop in the vegetable patch behind the stable and had offered the Blacks a good portion of them. Often the Laymans and the Blacks would exchange gifts of foods—beans, corn, fish, mutton—if there was more than enough for one family. Patsy didn't mind the work this morning because it was outside, and for once, the air was cool and pleasant. But she wished Barbara was helping her. Patsy had such a tale to tell! The red-haired stranger hadn't written the note about the fire. There was some other culprit responsible for Mr. Norris's terrible loss.

Patsy and the Declaration

The night before, after Mr. Black had bid his family good night, Patsy had shown him the note she'd found in the bushes. At first he chided her for playing a game with him. But then, after studying the small piece of paper, he grew quiet and serious, putting the note in his waistcoat pocket.

"Thank you, daughter, for bringing this to me," he'd said. "I will handle the matter. It should be no concern of yours."

This was a relief to Patsy. The scare she'd received in the stranger's bedchamber was enough to make her think the Daughters of Liberty would be better off with safer tasks. To imagine herself swinging from a British rope made her lungs freeze and her arms break out in cold sweat.

Katherine stuck her head out of the kitchen door. Her face was flushed with the heat from the huge oven. "How are you doing? Are the beans done? I would like to cook them with pork for this afternoon's dinner."

"I have quite a bit left," Patsy said. "If Barbara was here, she could help me. But she went with her mother to Boxler's Milliner and won't be back until evening."

"Can you find Nicholas, then? He knows how to prepare beans."

"He has gone chopping wood behind the stable," Patsy said.

"I see," Katherine said. "And the Andersons seem to have their hands full."

Patsy looked over at the bench by the well. Both ladies were at work boiling soap. One stoked the fire beneath the pot, the other stirred carefully. These ladies were so quiet and so serious, Patsy found them a challenge. She tried many times to get the ladies to smile or chuckle by telling jokes or singing silly songs, but they remained serious and true to their tasks.

"Well, then. Just snap as quickly as you can," Katherine said. "Have them to me in ten minutes and there's a slice of cheese for you."

Patsy forced her fingers to move more quickly— pick up a bean, snap off the ends, pull the string and drop it into the bowl on the ground.

A shadow fell across Patsy's lap and she looked up. Barbara stood in front of her, her arms crossed, a frown on her face.

"Hello!" Patsy said. "You are back early from the shop."

"I'm back for good," Barbara said. She kicked at a clump of grass. "Mrs. Boxler said my mother and I weren't to return."

Patsy and the Declaration

The bowl nearly slid from Patsy's lap. "What? Why not? Your mother is the clerk. She is needed there. Did you do something awful?"

"No, of course not!" Barbara said. "It is business, Mrs. Boxler said. There is not enough trade now to keep my mother on as help. Mrs. Boxler said she and Abby will have to try to keep the shop open on their own."

Patsy took a deep breath, then reached for her friend's hand. "I'm so sorry," she said. "I know your mother liked working at the shop."

"It's not just that," Barbara said. She sat down in the grass beside the bowl of beans. "We will have less money now. My mother must find employment elsewhere."

Patsy tried to sound cheerful. "Oh, that shouldn't be difficult. Your mother is a wise woman with many skills. She should be accepted in many a shop."

"I hope so," Barbara said. She pulled a blade of grass from the ground, stuck it in her mouth and chewed on it for a moment. Then she said, "Would you like help with the beans?"

Patsy nodded and scooted over on the wooden bench to give her friend room. Patsy counted slowly to fifty, giving her friend time to be sad about her mother's employment. Then it was time for the news.

"The tall stranger didn't set the fire," she said in a low voice.

This perked Barbara up. Her eyes grew wide and the smile returned. "Certainly? How do you know? Tell me what you did to find out. Oh, tell me everything that happened last night!"

"I dressed in Henry's clothes and sneaked upstairs."

"You didn't!"

"I did."

"Patsy, you are a Daughter of Liberty to be certain. Tell me more."

"I found the man's room and a letter he was writing. It is not the same script."

"He's not a spy?"

"I don't think so."

"Barbara!" It was Katherine again, coming from the kitchen with a basketful of bread on her hip. "Thank you for helping Patsy. I'll have some cheese for both of you when you're finished." Katherine crossed the yard to the tavern's back door. As she pulled the door open, Mr. Norris's apprentice, Randolph, came outside. He pulled

his hat down to shade his eyes and passed Patsy
and Barbara without speaking.

But Patsy wouldn't let rudeness pass by. "Good
morning, Randolph."

The young man grumbled, "Good morning,"
but nothing more, and he continued down the dirt
path toward the stable and the burned building.

"Why is he here today?" Barbara asked, putting a bean tip between her teeth. "Mr. Norris
has gone off to find other work, and there is nothing for Randolph here but ashes."

"I suppose he just wants to take another look,"
Patsy said. "He feels very bad about the fire."

Barbara spit out the chewed-up bean tip. "Perhaps he is. But there is nothing left for him to see."

"We visit my grandmother's grave. There's
nothing to see there, either, but a stone."

Barbara shook her head and stood up. "He was
looking strange, don't you think? Let's follow
him. Let's go see what he is up to."

"Why?"

"Let's just do."

"We can't. We have to finish these beans
right away."

"No, you have to finish the beans. I don't. I'll
go alone if you don't want to."

Exasperated, Patsy said, "No, I don't want to."

"Then wait for me. I'll be back soon," Barbara said. And she ran off down the path after Randolph.

Katherine came out of the tavern, the bread basket empty. She wiped her forehead with her wrist and said, "Where did Barbara go?"

"Mad," Patsy said, shaking her head. "She went utterly mad! Like her mother often says, 'I don't know what to make of the girl at times.' "

Katherine chuckled and went back inside the kitchen. After snapping the rest of the beans, Patsy carried the bowl to Katherine, who already had water and fat boiling. The smell was wonderful. The beans went into the pot and the lid went on top. Then Katherine and Patsy sat down at the table and each took a large chunk of cheese from the wheel. The texture was smooth and the taste creamy. Patsy chewed for a few moments before talking. Then she said, "Katherine, what would you do if you couldn't work here anymore?"

"Why?" Katherine asked with a wink. "Is your father looking to be free of me?"

"No," Patsy said. "But is employment hard to find in Philadelphia now?"

"Why do you ask?"

"Barbara's mother can't work at the milliner's now because business is bad."

"Oh," Katherine said, patting Patsy's arm and dipping her a mug of cool water from the bucket by the table. "Mrs. Layman is a clever woman. She'll be fine."

"The Laymans moved here from the country three years ago to find a good living. Now I'm afraid they might have to move all over again. If Barb left, I'd cry so much. She's my best friend."

"Don't worry," Katherine said. "True friends remain so even if distance comes between them. That's something I've learned. Many of my friends have moved to other places, but we still write letters and are still friends."

Barbara suddenly appeared in the kitchen doorway. Her eyes were huge with excitement. "Patsy, you won't believe it! Come quickly!"

"Why?" Patsy asked.

"Shh, and come here!"

Patsy went to the door. Barbara leaned in close to her ear. "I know who burned the blacksmith's shop. Now we must follow him to his place of hiding."

8

"Why would Randolph burn the shop?" Patsy asked as she ran after Barbara to the stable. "It makes no sense at all!"

"Yes, it does. He got Mr. Norris's trust, and then turned on him. He supports the Crown and Mr. Norris refused to. We must hurry if we are to watch his movements. He went down the alley."

"I gave my father the note, Barb. I think this is better off in adult hands, not ours!"

"Stop fussing! Daughters of Liberty are brave and smart. We can do this. Once we know where he goes and where he stays and with whom he works, we'll tell our fathers. Then they can have the arsonists arrested."

"We can't prove anything!"

"I think we can!"

"If you're right," Patsy said as they reached the stable, "then we must move quickly. Let's take your pony."

"Good thinking!"

Little Bit was standing in the paddock, grazing on stray bits of hay, her bridle draped over a fence post. Barbara snatched up the bridle and secured it on the pony in a flash. She led the pony through the gate and locked it quickly. With one hop, she was on Little Bit's back.

"Come on!" Barbara held her hand out for her friend. Patsy took hold and was pulled up onto Little Bit's back behind Barbara. She wrapped her arms around Barbara's waist as her friend tapped her heels into the pony's ribs. Patsy's skirt was bunched beneath her, and her stockings were slippery against the pony's sides.

"Whoa!" Patsy cried as the pony broke into a brisk canter, past the stable and into the alleyway behind the tavern. She heard Mrs. Layman shout from an upstairs stable window, "Barbara, where are you going? Barbara, did you hear me?" But Barbara didn't look back or slow the pony down.

Little Bit's hooves scrambled in the sharp turn

and he stumbled, but righted himself and ran on. "Be careful!" cried Patsy. "I'll go off!"

Barbara only leaned over Little Bit's neck, gripping the reins tightly, and said, "Hold on, Patsy!"

They raced into the street and Barbara drew the pony up, looking right and left to find Randolph. She pointed. The young man was already two blocks ahead and moving at a rapid clip. "There he is! Now, we'll slow down and keep to his rear. He has friends, I'm certain. Randolph would never think of burning the shop on his own. We want to know where his nest of spies gathers."

"It makes me sad to think he is the one," Patsy said. "He always seemed so nice."

"He *is* the one," Barbara said.

Patsy braced her legs against the pony's sides to keep from sliding, but it was nearly impossible. He was so slick. *How does Barbara do it?* she wondered.

The girls rode down the street, staying to the edge, gathering amazed glances from everyone they passed. *They don't approve of two girls riding so,* Patsy thought. *Well, that doesn't matter now. Let them stare!*

"Tell me," Patsy said, leaning over Barbara's

shoulder, watching Randolph as he walked a half block ahead of them. "What makes you think Randolph set the fire?"

"He was gazing at the burned remains of the shop. I asked him if he would wait a moment, I had a favor to ask him. He hesitated but agreed. So I went up to my room and brought down a piece of paper, ink and pen. I told him I wanted to write a letter to my grandmother in Boston, Massachusetts, but didn't know how to spell either word. I said my father and mother were too busy to help me."

"And?"

"And I asked if he would write it for me."

"He said yes?" Patsy asked.

"At first he said no. Then I told him that was all right, I knew a blacksmith's apprentice didn't have the education to write and spell. This made him angry and he snatched the paper right up!"

"He's gone left," Patsy said. Barbara slowed the pony even more and stopped at the intersection of Mulberry and Seventh Street. Barbara and Patsy peeked around the corner. The young man was still walking with his brisk stride. He seemed to have no idea that he was being followed.

"So you have the paper?" Patsy said.

"Yes, here." Barbara drew the folded sheet from her skirt and gave it to Patsy. The handwriting was the same as on the note. The *m* matched, with rounded peaks, and the *s*'s were the same, too, curling down below the other letters and ending in a looping swirl. The hairs on Patsy's neck and arms stood up. Randolph Bonner had, indeed, written the note she'd found.

Barbara urged Little Bit ahead. They passed a cooper's shop, with its yard full of barrels and tools and scraps of wood, and the clock maker's, with its window display of various time pieces.

And then Randolph went into a shop on the right. Barbara guided Little Bit to a post across the street and dismounted.

"We must watch his every move," Patsy murmured.

"Yes," Barbara said.

Patsy slid off the pony without looking. Her feet came down in a fresh pile of manure. "Vexation!" she said.

"Stop complaining," Barbara said. "Wipe your shoes off and come on. We might have our answer right here." She hurried across the street, dodging the traffic.

The place was a print shop. The wooden sign

over the door, waving in the warm breeze, read, ROBINSON'S PRINT SHOP AND POST OFFICE. The girls stopped and shaded their eyes, peering in the window from the very edge so as not to be noticed. At first all Patsy could see were the goods in the shop—shelves of stationery, slates and pencils, ink and inkhorns, sealing wax, spectacles, quills and coffee. She squinted and pressed her nose harder into the glass.

Randolph was near a door in the back, talking with two other men, both older. One man, with a black wig, shifted from one foot to the other as if he was nervous. He kept rubbing his chin and picking at one of the brass buttons on his blue waistcoat. The other, an old man with white hair and a gray waistcoat, crossed his arms and frowned, nodding his head as if every word Randolph said was very important. The more Randolph talked, the more animated he became. His arms moved around, his shoulders went up and down.

And then the man in the gray waistcoat reached out and slapped Randolph soundly on the cheek. Randolph flinched, moved back a step and stopped talking. The man put his finger in Randolph's face and jabbed it several times, saying

★ 99 ★

something with obvious anger. Randolph hung his head and listened.

"I wish I knew what they were saying," Patsy whispered.

"Shhh!" Barbara warned. "And come with me."

There was a narrow alley beside the shop. The girls crept around to a side window, which was opened halfway. Next to the window, with Patsy standing straight and Barbara kneeling down, they could hear the conversation inside.

"So," came the old man's scratchy voice, "Norris didn't find the note. He has said nothing about it to you or anyone else? Being careless is as bad as being a traitor, Randolph."

Randolph said, "I don't know how the note got lost, but it did. I believe it burned up."

"Then the fire was useless. All that planning and all that care, and all anyone can determine is that the fire was an accident! An accident! Can you hear how that sounds, Bonner? Norris was supposed to find the note, read it and share it with his friends. This way, they would all know what folly it is to ignore requests to help the soldiers of the King. They would all know that if a request came for their aid to the Crown, they best find a way to honor the request or they, too, might lose their homes or shops or possessions."

"I know," Randolph said. "I went to put another note at the remains of Norris's shop today. I came through the tavern without being noticed, as there were so many men and so much activity. But outside, one of the hired girls saw me and struck up conversation."

"Hired girl? Hah! I dare him to call me a hired girl to my face. I am the stable manager's daughter, not a hired girl," Barbara whispered. Patsy nudged her friend to keep her quiet.

"If I'd left a note, she surely would have traced it to me," Randolph continued.

"You think a hired girl is that smart?" The man slapped Randolph again. The blow left a red streak across his face. "You are not to think, you are to do as you are told. Is that clear, Mr. Bonner?"

"Yes, sir."

"Well, boy," said the old man, "Paul Templeton at the gunsmith's has also refused to help the King. A private request for gun repairs and supplies for our army only brought from Templeton a scowl and laugh. He must know that it is to his peril that he chooses to be neutral in the war. Here is your last chance, Randolph. A little heat. A little note, where the gunsmith will find it. Then others in Philadelphia will think twice about following the teachings of Thomas Paine or those savages at the State House who promote independence."

"This time, I will be most careful," Randolph said.

The girls heard the sound of footsteps moving toward the front door. They clamored away from the window and stood with their backs to the street, pretending to stare down the alley at a stack of crates. Patsy could barely breathe. Her lungs ached with fear and excitement.

I hope he doesn't notice us!

Several seconds later, Barbara tugged on her sleeve. "He's gone off again, heading west. Let's follow! We must know his every move." Barbara grabbed Patsy's hand and nearly dragged her back to Little Bit. With a leg up, Patsy found herself once more behind her best friend, clinging on for dear life as the pony picked up a trot.

"Slow down or he'll see us for certain," Patsy said into her friend's ear. "He knows your pony. He knows us!"

Barbara brought Little Bit down to a brisk

walk. They followed the apprentice down several more blocks, crossing High Street and passing George Clark's famous coachmaking shop. Little Bit seemed to sense the adventure of the moment and wanted to trot instead of walk. Barbara kept a steady grip on the reins.

Then Randolph slowed and paused in front of the gunsmith's shop. He stood staring at the door, his arms to his side, his fists clenched. Patsy felt afraid for herself, but for Randolph, too. Did he realize what he was doing? Did he really believe it was right?

Barbara guided Little Bit behind a wagon, and the girls sat quietly, waiting to see what the young man was going to do. Randolph looked up and down the street, then went inside the shop. Barbara and Patsy slipped from Little Bit's side, tied his reins to a light post and walked slowly in the direction of the shop.

"If he is going to set a fire there, we must let someone know before there is any damage," Barbara said.

"We can't accuse him of doing something he hasn't done," Patsy said. "He might not have the chance to do as he plans, or he might even change his mind. If he comes out and we've shouted 'fire!'

it is we who will be the fools, and no one will listen to anything we say after that."

"I'm not sure you are right."

"Just hush and wait."

But no sooner did they near the gunsmith's window than Randolph was coming out, walking hastily with his hat tugged low over his eyes.

He's coming our way! Patsy thought, and as she did, Randolph passed the girls. He looked up and stared directly at Patsy.

"Oh," Patsy said in horror.

"Oh!" Randolph said. His face twisted in fear and sadness. Then he broke into a run. He fled down the street and disappeared among the pedestrians and wagons.

Patsy grabbed Barbara's sleeve and exclaimed, "He saw me! He knows we followed him!"

"But look there!" Barbara pointed in through the window of the gunsmith's shop. From behind a short stack of wooden boxes in the shop's corner, a small tendril of smoke could be seen rising like a curly gray ribbon.

Randolph had set the gunsmith's shop on fire!

9

"Fire!" Patsy screamed to the people on the street. "Fire! There's a fire at the gunsmith's shop!"

Immediately several men raced from the street and pushed through the door into the shop. Women and children flocked to the windows and door, trying to peer in and see what was happening. Patsy and Barbara were pushed back into the road.

"I can't see," Barbara said.

"We must get through," Patsy said. "We need to talk to the shop owner. We need to find Randolph's note!" Using her shoulders, she forced her way up to the door. One man said, "Get back, girl!" but Patsy answered, "I must talk with Mr. Templeton! I know who set the fire!"

The man ignored her. He shouted through the door, "Is it out? Is the fire done with?"

From inside, a man called, "Yes, thank God. It was caught quickly. There are only some boxes scorched."

"Mr. Templeton!" Patsy called over the small crowd. "Mr. Templeton, I must speak with you right away! I know who did this!"

Men stared down at Patsy, suddenly silent. A portly man with thick eyebrows and a scar on his cheek came out of the door and stood before Patsy. He was sweating heavily. He held a crumpled note in his hands.

"You found the note!" Patsy said. "I know who left it, sir!"

"Girl? You say you know something about this? Did you or your little friend there set the fire as a prank while I was in the back room?"

"No, sir! No prank. I tell you the truth."

"I found this note here," Mr. Templeton said, shoving the note at Patsy. "You knew about the note!"

"What does the note say?" asked a bystander.

"It is a warning that I must lose my shop for not helping the King's army!"

There were "ahhs" and "oohs" from the crowd.

Mr. Templeton stooped down and snarled, "Did you write this note, child?"

But Patsy stood straight, staring the man directly in the eye. She would not let him scare her. "No, sir. But I saw the man who went in and came out, leaving the fire and the note behind."

"Then who was it?"

Patsy hesitated. She knew she had to give Randolph's name, but sadness caught her throat and made it difficult to talk. She'd always liked Randolph. He'd never had anything but a smile for her as she'd peeked into Mr. Norris's shop. But he had done a bad thing. She had to pass the information on. "Randolph," she managed. "Randolph Bonner. He is just down the street a little ways. He is young, about twenty, in brown clothing. He is apprenticed to our blacksmith, Roger Norris, at Black's Tavern."

Most of the men, with shouts of anger, ran down the street after Randolph. Mr. Templeton waddled after them. The women stayed in a cluster and spoke to each other in hushed defiant tones. Children stared between the shop and the twelve-year-old girl who had known the villain.

"It's time to go home," Patsy said to Barbara. "We must share your evidence with our fathers and let them deal with this now."

Barbara nodded. She seemed a little sad, too. What would happen to Randolph? It was dreadful to think about.

Little Bit was digging dusty holes in the side of the street with her hoof. She nickered when she saw Barbara and waved her head back and forth. Wearily the girls dragged themselves onto the pony and rode back to Black's Tavern.

At the stable, they were met by Mrs. Layman and Mrs. Black. The women had hands on their hips, and both looked furious and frightened.

"What were you doing?" Mrs. Layman said. "Barbara, I called you and you ignored me! Racing off like a phantom on that pony, when the two of you had chores."

"You scared us so," Mrs. Black said. "Patsy, what were you thinking?"

The girls dropped from the pony's back. They ran to their mothers and gave them big hugs. "I'm sorry I scared you," Patsy said, and then no one said anything for what seemed like a very long time.

Then Patsy stepped back and said, "Barbara and I have something we must show Father. Is he in the tavern?"

Mr. Black was in the tavern, sitting in the Ulysses Room with several other men whom Patsy knew to be his closest friends. They were playing cards. There were men at other tables, smoking, sipping ale and talking. When Mr. Black saw the women with such serious faces and the girls with wrinkled and horsehair-covered dresses, he left his table and strode over.

"Has something happened?" he asked.

"It has indeed," Mrs. Black said. "Ask Patsy."

Mr. Black knelt down in front of Patsy and took one of her hands in his. A strand of hair had fallen down over his forehead. His dark eyes were bright and serious. "What is it, daughter?"

Patsy spoke quietly so the other men in the room couldn't hear. "Barbara and I know who set the fire in Mr. Norris's shop. We have proof. It was Randolph."

"Not the apprentice, Randolph Bonner?" Mr. Black asked.

"Yes, sir," Barbara said. "The very same."

Patsy continued. "The note I gave you the other evening matches the handwriting on a note Randolph wrote for Barbara. We followed him and found his friends at Robinson's print shop. We heard them talking about scaring people into helping the King win the war. Then we saw him go into the gunsmith's. He set another fire, Father."

Mr. Black stood straight. He took a deep breath, glanced at his daughter, his wife, Barbara and Mrs. Layman. Then he said, "I never wanted to get involved in the war, you know that. I have had loss because of it. But this is in my hands now, isn't it? I have nothing to do but tell the authorities and let them do what they must."

He went to his friends, spoke with them a moment, and Patsy could hear one say, "We will go with you, Andrew. The children did a good thing."

Mr. Black came back over to Patsy, leaned over and took her in a warm tight embrace. Then he said, "Thank you, Patsy. You are indeed brave. Because of your actions, the fires will stop and the shops will be saved."

"You are welcomed," Patsy said. She looked at Barbara. It was then she realized how truly dirty they both were and how messy they looked. She burst into giggles. She and Barbara laughed until their sides ached, and their mothers led them off to find a clean change of clothes.

Though it was not yet dark, Patsy became tired enough to go to bed. The side garden was still bathed in evening sunlight, and Dorcas was in the yard with Mrs. Black, who was talking with Katherine about the next day's meals. Henry had taken Nicholas for a walk. Barbara was back with her family on the second floor of the stable.

Patsy pulled out her trundle bed and dropped down, removed her shoes and stockings and stretched out her legs. On the floor, the shadows of tree branches moved back and forth, friendly gray ghosts gently caressing the rug.

From under her pillow Patsy pulled the newspaper the stranger from Virginia had given her. The paper was dated March 20, 1776. She opened it and found a poem by a woman named Phillis Wheatley. The poem's title was "A Hymn to the Evening."

"Soon as the sun forsook the eastern main,
The pealing thunder shook the heav'nly plain;
Majestic grandeur! From the zephyr's wing,
Exhales the incense of the blooming spring."

These words were soothing and lovely. It made the troubles of the day seem far away. She lay down, wriggled her head against her pillow and read on.

"Let places slumbers sooth each weary mind,
At mourn to wake more heav'nly, more refin'd;
So shall the labours of the day begin
More pure, more guarded from the snares of sin."

Patsy smiled and put the newspaper on the bed beside her. What a fine woman, to write with such insight.

Perhaps someday I shall try my hand at poetry, Patsy thought. *I don't know of what I would write, but to have wonderful things to say in print must be fine, indeed.*

The bedroom door eased open. Mr. Black came in and sat on the chair, looking at his daughter. He took off his tri-cornered hat and held it in his hands, turning it around and around.

"I am proud of you," he said finally.

Patsy sat up. "Thank you, Father."

"You have courage to do what you think is right."

"So do you, Father. You've always been brave

enough to do what you need to do and stand strong because of it. It is your example that has taught me to be what I am."

Mr. Black smiled broadly, then said, "What are you reading?"

"A copy of the *Virginia Gazette*. I found a poem by a lady named Phillis Wheatley. She tells about the beauty of the evening."

"Do you like the poem?"

Patsy nodded.

"Then I have something else you might enjoy." Mr. Black opened the family's trunk and brought out a copy of the *Pennsylvania Magazine*. "I recognize the poet's name. Read, and then get some sleep. You deserve a good rest." He gave his daughter a long warm hug and then ruffled her blond hair. With a wink, he collected his hat and left the room.

Patsy thumbed through the magazine and came upon "To His Excellency, General Washington."

"Celestial choir! enthron'd in realms of light,
Columbia's scenes of glorious toils I write.
While freedom's cause her anxious breast alarms,
She flashes dreadful in refulgent arms.

See mother earth her offspring's fate bemoan,
And nations gaze at scenes before unknown."

The poem continued, telling of the brave country and her battle for freedom under the command of the glorious General Washington. Patsy closed the magazine and thought, *Maybe I can write of what I am learning, of the need for freedom for everyone. Freedom from unfair government, freedom from fear, freedom from danger.*

She looked at the small table and at the ink well and paper sitting there. "I should like to write a poem!" she said. But before she could even imagine the first line of her poem, her eyelids closed and she dropped back onto the mattress. In only a moment, she had drifted into a deep peaceful slumber.

10

"I feel sorry for Randolph," Patsy said to Katherine. They were in the kitchen. Both stood at the table with bowls full of dough, pounding it with their fists to make biscuits. It was just after noon. The preparations for the tavern's four-o'clock meal had just begun.

"Why do you feel sorry for the boy?" Katherine asked. "He did a terrible thing. Mr. Norris has moved in with his son across the city until he can rebuild his shop, if indeed he finds he can afford it. The damage at Mr. Templeton's gunsmith shop was small, but it could have been much worse. I feel no pity for Randolph."

"The fires were dreadful," Patsy said. She

scratched at her nose with her knuckle, leaving a streak of flour. "But Randolph is young and was misled by clever scheming men into arson. Randolph truly believes in the cause of the King and thought it was the right thing to do."

"Many people use excuses such as that," Katherine said. "They do terrible things for a cause in which they believe."

"But killing is terrible," Patsy said. "And a war kills people, from battles to sickness to hangings. A war is fought for a cause, isn't it?"

Katherine stopped pounding her dough and gave Patsy a sad smile. "I suppose it is, Patsy."

"Do all men who want independence from the King also want war?"

Katherine seemed to ponder this. She pounded the dough a bit more, then sighed and looked out through the open door. "I think no good man truly wants war. It only comes when there is no other option."

"George Washington doesn't want to fight?"

"I think he would rather settle the disagreement with the King peacefully. Who would prefer loss of life and limb and family? But the King will not listen to rational talk. It just doesn't seem possible to solve this without a fight."

"I wish it was possible."

"So do I. So do most people. But who can truly know about such things?"

"Someone should know," Patsy said. "Someday someone should figure it out."

The two pounded the dough in silence for a while, then Patsy said, "I would like to do something nice for someone today. I've had enough of bad things. A cheerful task would lighten the day."

"Who do you have in mind?"

"The men at the State House, the members of the Continental Congress. It is such a hot dreadful day. I think they would appreciate something tasty to eat and something cool to drink."

"I think that's a wonderful idea," Katherine said. "When we are done with the dough and I have the biscuits cooking, ask your mother if you may."

Patsy pounded twice as fast, and her hands flew as she helped Katherine press out and roll the biscuits. Then she ran into the tavern, where she found her mother sitting in the bedroom with Dorcas and Mrs. Brubaker.

"Hello, Miss Black," Mrs. Brubaker said, nodding politely in her chair and waving a fan at her cheeks. "It is nice to see you today."

"Thank you, ma'am," Patsy said. "Mother, I would like to do something for the members of the Continental Congress."

"Gracious, what?" asked her mother. "After the daring adventure you and young Barbara had, are you now planning on taking up arms and joining the fight?"

Patsy shook her head. "I would like to take them something to eat and drink. They are working hard for us; I think we could do something for them."

"My, my," Mrs. Brubaker said. She lowered the fan and touched a gloved finger to her lips. "Girls should not be so active in the affairs of men. Rebecca, do you encourage your daughter to step outside what is acceptable for young ladies?"

But Mrs. Black smiled and said, "I find my daughter has a mind of her own. She has a good and stout heart and for the most part makes wise choices. Patsy, you may take the food."

"Thank you!" Patsy gave her mother a hug. Then she looked at Mrs. Brubaker, who, surprisingly so, was not frowning. Instead, she said,

"Wear your bonnet, dear. You do not want to lose your lovely complexion."

"I will," Patsy said. And without thinking, she leaned over and gave Mrs. Brubaker a hug. Mrs. Brubaker hesitated, then hugged her back. As Patsy curtsied, put on her bonnet and left the room, she thought she noticed a tear in the old woman's eye.

She skipped to the stable, where she found Barbara sitting on the paddock fence, weaving a braid on a tape-loom. The braid, which was long and nearly touching the ground, could be used for many things, such as glove ties, stay laces, and hatbands.

"Good morning!" Barbara said.

"Good morning! What are you making?"

"Oh, just an old hair lace. I can do this later. Do you have time to play?"

"No, but I have a chore for the Daughters of Liberty."

Barbara wrinkled her nose. "Chore? I have had enough of those for a while."

"A fun chore, Barb. We'll take a meal to the members of Congress at the State House. My mother has given me permission."

"That's a fine idea," Barbara said. She rolled

up the braid and jumped down from the fence. "I'll take this upstairs and ask my mother if I may go, too."

In only a minute, Barbara was back down, tying her bonnet around her chin. "My mother said she was surprised I asked about going, but was glad I did. What are we going to take?"

"Let's see what we have in the kitchen that looks tasty."

Katherine had already set a large basket out on the kitchen table and lined it with a clean linen towel. She waved the girls in and said, "What shall we send our fine men?"

After taking inventory of the prepared food on the table and shelves, the basket was filled with biscuits, a large bowl of cool custard, dried figs, almonds, beef, slices of ham and raisins. A second towel was draped over the basket to keep flies off the food. Patsy paused just outside the gate of the side garden to pick several golden dandelions and two bright red roses to brighten up the top of the basket. Each girl then picked a single rose, snapped off the thorns, and wove the flower into the brim of their bonnet. Then they set off for Chestnut Street.

Patsy and the Declaration

They sang flower songs as they walked, swinging the basket between them.

> "Dandelion, the globe of down,
> The schoolboy's clock in every town,
> Which the truant puffs amain
> To conjure back long hours again."

Abby was at the milliner door, beating the dirt from a small rug draped over the stoop's railing. Patsy and Barbara waved as they passed her by. They continued singing:

> "On a summer's day in sultry weather,
> Five brethren were born together,
> Two had beards, and two had none,
> And the other had but half a one!"

As the girls neared the entrance to a baker's shop, the door banged open and an old man stumbled out into the street. The shopkeeper stood at the door, waving a fist at the man.

"Do not return, you beggar! I've had enough of your pitiful countenance. It scares away my good paying customers! Be off with you or I'll find a rock to urge you on your way!"

The door slammed shut.

The old man pulled his hat from his head, rubbed his bristly face with his hand, and sat down on the step of the shop. He mumbled to himself and picked at a loose thread on the hat's brim.

Patsy slowed her walking. Barbara cast her a confused look.

"We should help him," Patsy said.

"How?"

"The man is hungry. Daughters of Liberty want freedom for everyone, don't we? He is not free from hunger. Hunger is a very bad thing."

Barbara seemed to ponder this for a second, then smiled. "Yes. We have a great deal of food in our basket. Certainly we can spare a bit."

As they approached the man, he looked up as if he were afraid the girls were going to strike him. But Patsy knelt down and said, "Sir, if you would like, we have extra biscuits and ham. It makes our basket too heavy, and you would help us to take some."

The man sat a little straighter, and he tried to smooth the sleeves and collar of his tattered waistcoat. "Well, ladies, I should be happy to help you unburden the basket."

Barbara took three biscuits and a large slice of ham from beneath the towel. The man took it as carefully and as gracefully as any gentleman.

"Thank you, young ladies," he said. "And God bless you."

Patsy and Barbara curtsied and continued along the street. A block past the baker's shop, they heard crying over the sound of squeaking wagon wheels and whinnying horses. Barbara stopped and tilted her head. "Do you hear that?" she asked.

Patsy nodded. "A child's cry. Someone is hurt."

The girls turned around and around in the street, looking for the source of the sound. A man on horseback shouted at them as he rode by at a fast trot, "Get out of the way, children! The middle of the road is not for play!"

"Look there!" Barbara was pointing to a shaded corner of a cooper's yard. Sitting in the shade between several large hogsheads was a little boy of no more than ten years. The boy had his knees drawn up to his chin, and his face was buried in his hands.

The girls carried the basket over to the boy, and he looked up. His eyes were red with weeping.

"Go away," he said. "I've had enough teasing!"

"Teasing?" Patsy said. "Why would we tease you?"

"My father's crimes are not mine. I have never stolen so much as a nail or button."

Barbara cast Patsy a look of concern, and both girls squatted down to talk to the boy directly.

"Is your father a thief?" Barbara asked.

The boy nodded slowly. He stared at the girls with narrow eyes, as if he would bolt from the place any second. "He is in the jail, and you know that. You've just come over to chide me."

"No," Patsy said. "We don't know your father. We heard you crying and thought there might be something we could do to help."

"No one can help. My mother is dead and my little sister and I live wherever we can find a place to sleep. Now, leave me be."

"You have no parents to care for you?" Patsy asked.

The boy shook his head. "But I'm nine and I can work. Leave me be."

"Where is your sister?"

The boy scowled. "I shan't tell you. You leave her alone!"

"Perhaps," Barbara said softly, "you would like something to eat?"

The boy jumped up and made to run, but then he turned back. "You are teasing me again. You want me to come close to you and then you'll slap and pinch me, like the others do."

"Here, then," Barbara said. She opened the basket, took out all the figs, raisins, the bowl of custard, four biscuits and some beef. She wrapped it all in one of the linen towels and put it on the ground at the boy's feet.

The boy's eyes went as wide and round as apples. "That is for my sister and me?"

"Yes," Patsy said. "Please take care of her. And if you need work, come by Black's Tavern on Mulberry Street. I might talk my father into finding a chore or two to be done for some shillings."

The boy glanced all around as if he were afraid the food on the ground was a trap. But then he snatched up the towel and raced away, his feet digging divots in the road.

"Freedom from worry, at least for a little while," Barbara said.

"Yes," said Patsy.

In a few minutes they arrived at Chestnut Street. The State House was large and plain, made of red brick. The middle section was two

stories high, with a belfry at the top. The west
and east wings were single stories. There was a
large, grassy lawn in front of the building. Citizens
had gathered about the lawn, some seated as if
on a picnic, some clustered near windows in the
eastern wing of the building, trying to listen in.
The girls skipped across the lawn to the large
door, but then Patsy tugged on the basket and
said, "Wait a moment."

"What?" Barbara asked.

"I think we should see what we have left in the
basket," Patsy said. "I'm afraid it won't be
enough for the Congress."

They peered inside, and indeed, the basket was
nearly empty. Only several biscuits, some ham
and beef slices lay at the bottom. A couple of
stray raisins rolled around inside.

"Not enough at all," Barbara said, her shoulders drooping. "We gave most of it away."

A loud booming voice split the air, coming
from the open windows. "Our patience is at its
end! What sane men can tolerate such pettiness?"

Another voice answered, "We've had enough
of your complaints, John. Sit down!"

Barbara and Patsy hurried to the window, joining a small crowd of men who stood in the grass,

heads tipped, listening. The girls put the basket on the ground and stood on tiptoe, trying to peer inside. But all they could see was the ceiling and the top of the walls.

"Can we do nothing but bicker?" came the first man's voice through the window. "You propose to tear down a masterpiece until it is nothing but scraps! The dreadful summer here in Philadelphia has baked your minds to mush!"

"Enough of you, John," said a third voice. "Find your seat and let us have our say!"

From behind Patsy came a softer voice, "Perhaps I can help."

She and Barbara spun about to see the tall red-haired stranger. He was standing on the grass not far from the assembly of curious citizens, with his hands tucked behind his back, his lavender waistcoat unbuttoned and the frills of his shirt wilted in the heat.

"Sir!" Patsy said. What was this man doing outside the State House? Had he followed the girls? Maybe he was the spy she had thought after all.

The man lifted a wooden bench from nearby and moved it beneath the window. "Now," he said, "you can better see how our Congress gentlemen conduct themselves. I fear that today you may not be very impressed." Then the man walked over to a nearby tree, slid down to the ground and linked his arms around his knees. He stared out at the street.

Patsy and Barbara hopped onto the bench, where they had a clear view of the men inside. Most sat at tables, others stood with arms crossed, while still others paced back and forth, shaking their heads and throwing their hands up. One man appeared to be sketching mindlessly on a piece of paper, looking as though he wished he were anywhere but in that room. Another man, standing at the head of the room, pounded his hand on a large table to get order, but the congressmen seemed to want nothing of it.

Patsy glanced back at the stranger beneath the tree. Then she climbed off the bench and walked over to him. Taking a deep breath, she asked, "What are you doing here, sir?"

The man raised one eyebrow. "Oh," he said. "I need a break from the drawing and quartering. The men inside that building are harsh critics, indeed."

"You know the men inside?"

A smile crept over the man's tired features. "Certainly, I do. I am one of them."

"You, sir?" Patsy couldn't believe her ears. "You are a member of the Continental Congress?"

The man laughed then, putting his head back against the tree's scabby trunk and holding his stomach as though it hurt. "Why, yes, dear lady," he said, "although some might consider it folly to admit such a thing. I have written a paper on behalf of the Congress, a paper about the freedoms due any man and any country. My fellow congressmen at this moment are debating its value. Some can find nothing good about it. My poor friend John Adams supports the paper, but continues to get into shouting matches where no one hears anyone else. I grew so tired and hungry that I was not able to listen any longer without anger. I came outside to take a break. Let them ramble on without me for a while."

A member of Congress! Patsy thought. Her ears felt flushed with embarrassment. She had thought this man a spy. He was a Patriot.

The basket sat in the grass beside the bench. As Barbara watched, Patsy picked it up and carried it to the gentleman. "There is little inside," she said. "But please enjoy it."

The man bowed slightly and then leaned back

against the tree and took a huge bite from a biscuit filled with ham.

"I'm sorry," Patsy said.

Around the mouthful he said, "For what?"

Patsy didn't know how to explain. So she said, "For lots of things."

When the man had finished his small meal, he stood under the tree, stretched, and said, "I think I'm better able to face them now." He went inside the State House. Patsy and Barbara put their hands on the windowsill and watched as the red-haired stranger strode inside the meeting room and took his place at a table near the front. He took a piece of paper, dipped a quill pen into an ink well and began to write.

"John Adams, you have heard nothing we've said here," said one tall man to a shorter one. "Will you never understand our concerns? The wording on the paper is too strong!"

"It is only strong enough!" Mr. Adams answered.

"We shall not ever agree on this."

But Mr. Adams said, "Everyone present has to come to an agreement, sir! On this, we must all hang together."

An old man, seated by the far wall with his

foot propped up on a stool, said, "Yes, we must indeed all hang together or most assuredly we shall all hang separately."

There were murmurs of agreement and disagreement through the meeting room.

Barbara nudged Patsy and said, "I wish I could be a congressman! What important things we could be doing."

Patsy smiled. "We are Daughters of Liberty. That is important, too."

The red-haired man stood up from his table and walked over to the open window. Without saying a word, he passed a folded note through to Patsy, then returned to his seat.

Patsy jumped from the bench and quickly opened the note. Barbara stood beside her, staring over her shoulder. "Read it!" she said. "What does it say?"

Patsy took a breath and read,

"July 1, 1776.

"Declaration. Be it known that Patsy Black has done a good deed for the cause of liberty by giving a much-needed meal to a humble member of the Continental Congress.

"Signed, Thomas Jefferson."

ABOUT THE AUTHOR

Elizabeth Massie was born, grew up, and still lives in the town of Waynesboro, Virginia. This town was named after the famous Revolutionary War general "Mad Anthony" Wayne, who wasn't born there, never lived there, and most likely never visited the town in his entire life. Ms. Massie was one of four children. Her mother, Patricia Spilman, is a well-known and award-winning watercolorist. Her father, Bill Spilman, ran the town's newspaper and drove a motorcycle with a sidecar. Ms. Massie always wanted to be a writer, but also wanted to be a secret agent, an actress, and a famous horseback rider. Maybe someday! She and her sister, Barbara Spilman Lawson, wrote the newly published picture book *Jambo, Watoto!* and are working on new book projects.

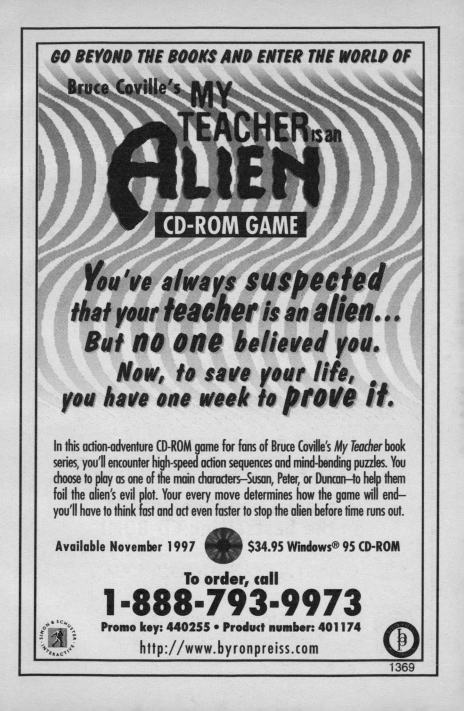